ARTAMA

& THE NEW KINGDOM

The Third Journey

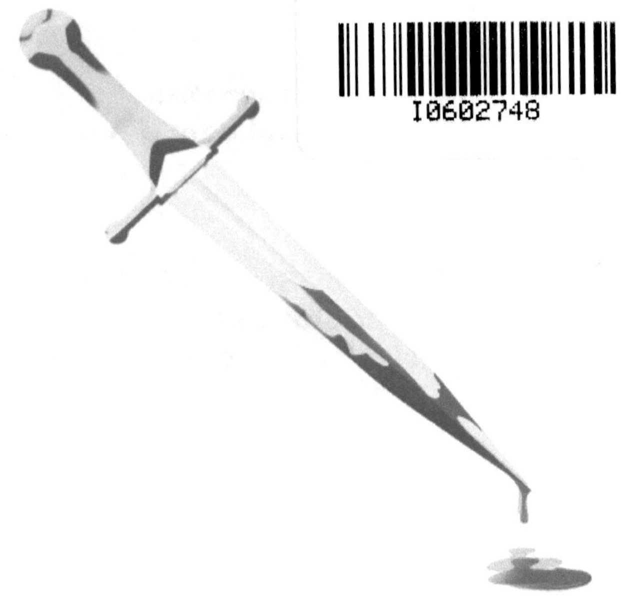

BRUCE PAUL

ARTAMA
& THE NEW KINGDOM
The Third Journey

© 2025 Bruce Paul
brucepaul.com

Cover design by **Stride Marketing Solutions**
Interior design by **Writer's Publishing House**

". . . Combining speculative fiction with deep philosophical undertones . . . ."

"Stellar world-building, dynamic pacing, and thought-provoking themes make this a must-read for fans of speculative fiction and fantasy."

"Through lyrical prose and a rich array of characters, Paul explores profound ideas about existence, fate, and the mysteries of the universe."

". . . Brilliant dialogue and interplay that contributes to the emotional depth and complexity . . . ."

"Themes of love, knowledge, betrayal, and the nature of life and death permeate the story."

". . . Robust characters, a fully drawn setting, and exciting prose. It is a gorgeous offering for fans of fantasy."

The Artama Legend series includes:

Artama & The Book of Knowledge & Wisdom
The First Journey

Artama & The Watchtower Portal
The Second Journey

Artama & The New Kingdom
The Third Journey

ARTAMA
& THE NEW KINGDOM
The Third Journey

Preface

THE ARTAMA LEGEND series began as a parable for children — *Artama & The Book of Knowledge & Wisdom* — followed by a novella for young adults — *Artama & The Watchtower Portal.*

The Prologue is for the benefit of those who have not read the first two books.

Prologue

THE ARTAMA LEGEND began before time.

Eventually, on planet E3, in The Town, at the edge of The Plain, Artama was born—a specific manifestation of the probabilistic.

Artama lived with his father, Alagon. Not long before Artama's birth, his father was the victim of an iniquitous disease. As a result, Alagon was blind.

Artama's mother died not long after his birth.

When the boy was old enough, he attended The Readings in The Hall with his father. The Readings were fundamental to the community, and — unquestioningly — the men gathered to listen to The Readers read from *The Book of Knowledge & Wisdom*.

Three Readers were seated at the front of The Hall, at a large table made of the wood of the weebon tree: The Reader in white, The Reader in black, and The Reader in gold—The Lord Most Honorable High Reader.

The Reader in gold read:

> Do not try to cross The Plain.
> There is no path—or food or water—
> Only dragon-fire — and dragon-
> slaughter.

In response, the men who crowded The Hall chanted, "It is written. It is true."

Artama noted that his father did not join the chant.

+++++

Alagon made pottery from the clay Artama dug from the riverbank on the edge of The Plain, and Artama painted colorful patterns on his father's work.

One morning, in the workshop, Artama was looking out the window, daydreaming. Artama turned toward his father and said, "I do not see dragon-fire. I see only the blue sky and the dust of The Plain." After a moment, he added, "I want to see for myself what is across The Plain."

Alagon responded, "I am old, and if I travel afar, it will be in your heart. I am blind, and if I see the far edge of The Plain, it will be through your eyes."

+++++

With his father's blessing, the following day, Artama began his journey. He carried a leather pack containing water, food, a tinderbox, and a needlebox. He wore a blanket as a cape.

Artama turned and looked back to the workshop.

His father was waving farewell.

Artama did not wave in return.

He walked east, onto The Plain, toward the dawn, toward the horizon—toward the unknown.

+++++

On the second night of his journey, sitting by his campfire—thirsty, hungry, and tired—Artama knew he was lost. He remembered words often read by The Reader in black:

When you are lost—and cannot

decide—

Let the needlebox be your guide.

The needlebox always points the

way home.

In the fading light, Artama saw his pack, gathered it, and felt inside. He found the needlebox and set it on a flat stone near the dying fire. Artama knew he could turn back now, but he remembered the words of his father: "I am old, and if I travel afar . . . ." Artama stared into the embers, and he saw the point of no return. He tightened his blanket around his shoulders.

+++++

There was a flash of blue and gold and white.

When he awoke, it felt like a dream.

Artama was looking out a window. The sky was blue—azure. In the sunlight, there was a garden and a golden fountain. Children were playing.

At the golden fountain, a lovely girl was filling a jar with water. The water was silver in the sunlight. When the jar was full, she stood and walked away, out of sight.

Artama looked around the room. He saw his pack on a table. Next to his pack was a cup. And next to the cup was a scarf, neatly folded. He heard a knock at the door.

A moment passed.

The door opened.

It was the girl.

She was holding the jar.

Smiling, she said, "I am Kora. I brought you water from the golden fountain."

Artama was smiling too. He looked out the window to the garden and the children and the fountain. Then, he looked again to Kora and said, "I am Artama." And, after a moment, he asked, "Where am I?"

"Across The Plain." Kora poured water into the cup.

Artama noted the bubbles. For a moment, they appeared, tended to gather and merge, and at last, they burst—becoming one with the air.

Kora unfolded the scarf, displaying a nutshell. She lifted the top, revealing a glowing amber ointment. "When you return, apply this to your father's eyes. He will see . . . they will *all* see."

Aloud, Artama wondered, "How am I here?"

"It is a matter of the heart."

+++++

There was a flash of blue and gold and white.

When Artama awoke, it felt like a dream.

The earth moving beneath his feet, Artama headed for home.

When, at last, he arrived at The Town, it was evening, the night of The Reading. He made his way to the open doorway of The Hall, where he stood and listened. The Lord Most Honorable High Reader read:

> Do not try to cross The Plain.
>
> There is no path—or food or water—
>
> Only dragon-fire — and dragon-
>
> slaughter.

And the other men chanted, "It is written. It is true."

Artama stepped forward. "It is *not* true!"

Everyone in The Hall turned to look at him.

He declared, "Although it is written, it is not true!"

Everyone was silent.

"I have crossed The Plain, and I have returned. I saw no dragon-fire. I saw no dragon-slaughter. Truly, it is a beautiful place."

There was tumult in The Hall.

The Reader in black shouted, "No one has ever crossed The Plain and returned!"

Artama removed the scarf from his pack and unfolded it. He took the nutshell, opened it, and walked to his father. First, Artama touched his finger to the ointment. Then, to his father's eyes.

A moment passed.

His father shouted, "I can see!"

Again, there was tumult in The Hall.

The Lord Most Honorable High Reader looked at the boy who had crossed The Plain and returned—and at the old blind man who could now see. He raised his hand, quieting the crowd. He said, "Young man—Artama—you are blessed. You have shown great courage, and you are wise beyond your years." After a pause, The Lord Most Honorable High Reader continued, "You shall be The Writer. You shall write words of knowledge and wisdom in *The Book of Knowledge & Wisdom*. Take this pen and write."

Artama turned to the first page in *The Book of Knowledge & Wisdom*, and he wrote: "Some of what is written is true."

+++++

Again, Artama and his father lived together.

One morning, there was a loud knock on the door, followed by an urgent cry: "Artama! Artama!" It was the runner of The Town. "The Readers sent me! You must come to The Hall at once!"

"Why?"

"I know only this: They are looking for you."

"*Who* is looking for me?"

The runner shuddered. "An unholy horde, an evil army." He wiped his mouth with the back of his hand to clean away the words.

"Why me?" But Artama already knew.

The runner shuddered again. "Because you know the way across The Plain. They think you can lead them to gold."

The myriad retellings of Artama's journey had been twisted into tales of unimaginable, material treasure.

And, now, Zortan and his beastly horde were at the edge of The Town, demanding that Artama lead them across The Plain, lead them to gold—or Zortan would burn down The Town.

In the crowded Hall, there was a great debate.

The Reader in black shouted at Artama, "Look what you have brought upon us!"

"This is all your fault, Artama!" echoed some in the crowd.

"Artama, help us!" cried others.

The Lord Most Honorable High Reader raised his hand, and The Hall fell silent.

Artama spoke, "I have a plan. I will agree to lead them onto The Plain, and I will lead them away."

The Reader in white said, "But if you lead them across The Plain, when they find what they want, they will plunder and waste. They will bring ruin, and they will kill you— they will need you no longer."

"I can lead them *onto* The Plain. But I will not lead them *across*." For Artama knew he could not: To journey across The Plain is a matter of the heart.

"But if they do not find what they want, they will *surely* kill you," said The Reader in white.

A wry smile crossed the face of The Reader in black.

The Reader in white reverently said, "Artama, you shall be remembered in story and song. Volumes shall be written about you."

The Reader in gold solemnly concluded, "Artama, I pray for you."

+++++

Artama walked to Zortan. There was an oily stench in the air. Heavy gold chains hung around Zortan's neck—gaudy, mismatched, and chaotic—tangled, twisted, and knotted. His face was disfigured by a terrible scar—a scar from fire—down his left temple and cheek. His left eye was partially closed by the damage. "I am Zortan!" He pounded his chest with his left fist. His war-horse, his huge black destrier, shifted. "I have been looking for you."

Artama simply stated, "I will lead you onto The Plain, but you must spare my people and my town."

Zortan chuckled. "Tell me, Artama, why must I spare your people and your town?"

"As a condition."

Zortan laughed. "You are in no position to set conditions. I will do as I please. I will take your head, drink your blood, and burn your town—leaving nothing but ashes."

"Then who will lead you to your destiny?"

Zortan stopped laughing. He turned toward the men behind him and commanded, "Take him! Shackle him!"

+++++

Artama led Zortan and his beastly horde aimlessly on The Plain.

On the second night, Artama witnessed The Game for the first time. He could walk to the end of the chain that trammeled him and see beyond Zortan's tent. He could see a circle of beastly men, and in the center of the ring was a young man wearing a black leather helmet with reptilian spikes—dragon-spikes—running down from the crown. He wore black leather gloves, and he crouched beside a blazing fire—red and orange and yellow. He was The Point—the point of injury and death— or, for the accomplished, the point of profit. A dirty black cloud boiled into the night. The beastly men in the circle fiercely threw glowing coals at the young man, and he batted them away—or caught them and threw them back in his own attack. The Fireman made his way furiously around the circle, carrying pots of glowing coals to the men who paid him well in gold. Gold coins, gold chains, and gold rings changed hands constantly. The beastly men wagered on everything.

Finally, after more aimless wandering, Zortan gave Artama an ultimatum: "Today is your last chance. Unless you show me something, we are turning back in the morning. I will proclaim it at The Game tonight. Some will be angry. Some will be relieved. They will *all* enjoy seeing you at The Point."

Only to delay, pointing, Artama said, "I need to climb that tower—to see—to get my bearings."

Zortan motioned for two guards and commanded, "Take him to his tower."

+++++

As Artama began to climb, the guards began throwing rocks. "Just practicing!" one shouted. "For The Game tonight!"

To the south, the sky became an angry red.

What could Artama hope for at the top of the tower?

He felt a sharp pain in his back.

Artama was now climbing for his life. He struggled to find holds and steps. A rock hit his right hand, almost costing him his grip. And then, in the cosmic moment when Artama turned his head, a rock hit, splitting open the center of his forehead—a bursting red star of torn flesh—sending blood swirling in the air. Artama could only endure. Beyond that, he was helpless. But if he endured, he could climb beyond the threat of the rocks, beyond the power of the guards. At last, he reached the top of the tower and crawled over a low wall of rocks on the rim. On the other side, he leaned back against the wall. Blood was running down onto his nose and cheeks. He wiped it away and wiped his bloody hand on his leg.

Finally, he was safe, and although he could hear the guards cursing, it was almost quiet, and he could think.

From the south, dragons began flying straight toward the tower—an undulating swarm of ancient, fire-breathing, reptilian creatures. Artama crouched among the rocks at the top of the tower and watched the swarm fly directly over him.

The first dragons were small, with keen red eyes. Their wings were translucent and fast—whining. These dragons were quick and agile. Smoke blew back from their nostrils, and fire torched from their mouths. Yet, their eyesight was their power.

Following the dragons with red eyes were larger dragons—dragons with yellow eyes. Their wings were thicker membranes. They, too, had flaming mouths, but their power was in their talons: brutal, ripping, shredding blades.

The whining became a deeper, humming despair.

Then came the true dragons of fire, dragons with blue eyes—gargantuan creatures that could produce almost invisible heat.

Artama watched in terror.

In the horde, The Last Man was the first man killed.

Zortan was riding furiously to the north when he was skewered by a falling banner standard and ripped from his horse. Writhing on the ground, heavy gold chains—gaudy, mismatched, and chaotic—tangled, twisted, and knotted—reflected the dragons' fire. He struggled to stand. A dragon with blue eyes torched him. Zortan ran, screaming. Another dragon torched him, and there was an explosion of putrefying vapors.

The enormous, blue-eyed dragons continued circling the burning beastly men, torching them with almost invisible heat. The fire became white. And then everything was gone. Nothing but ashes—the dust of The Plain.

A dragon flew straight toward Artama. Their eyes met. Artama did not move, and he did not blink. The dragon pulled back, hovered, and then flew away, off to the south, to rejoin the swarm.

+++++

Artama had no blanket, no water, no food. But today was the day it had to be, and he knew he was free.

In time, leaning against the low rock wall at the top of the tower, he fell asleep . . . into the blue and gold and white.

+++++

Artama heard the pure voices—the gorgeous harmony resonated and reverberated . . . . He could not recognize the voices, nor could he understand them. But he understood, nonetheless. He had no sense of time. He felt far away, far away from everything—except the voices. They were near him. They were inside him. He thought his eyes were closed. He knew they were not open. Yet he could see the colors of the chorus, the pure voices, the song everlasting, beyond the blue and gold and white. In the center of his forehead, Artama felt a soothing touch. He remembered the rock when it hit—heavy and sharp. His blood swirling in the air—bright and red. He felt a touch, and he inhaled a fragrance . . . a fragrance he knew . . . but could not name . . . redolent of miraculous healing. He could feel someone breathing. It was quiet. Nothing was ever quieter: the quiet of the moment before The Beginning, before the singularity. He saw only blue and gold now . . . and a black line curving, tipped with glowing orange. He realized he was staring at a candle flame. Artama heard the chorus again, and within the chorus, he heard his name. Now, he recognized a voice—*her* voice. The fragrance . . . the touch . . . . It was Kora! His forehead was suddenly radiant . . . with her kiss.

No longer a child, Kora had long, dark hair and deep, dark, eternal eyes. Her body was gracefully curved. She wore golden hoop earrings and a golden pendant—a talisman—a golden coin struck with the image of a dragon.

Artama felt a stirring he had never known before, and he knew he would never be the same.

He put his hand to his forehead, to the aching wound.

Knowingly, Kora said, "Your wound will heal. You will bear a scar, but it will be a radiant mark of honor."

In their conversation, Artama learned of The Academy, where he would study until the time for his return.

And Artama studied exhaustively, diligently, particularly the verisimilitudes. He studied Del't, the language of The Academy. He studied mathematics, physics, chemistry, biology, medicine, astronomy, navigation, cartography, philosophy, religion, meditation, astrology, literature, music, painting, sculpture, metallurgy, economics, politics, military strategy, martial arts, swordsmanship

. . . and Visioning. He studied comparative studies, and he studied the study of studies.

Artama studied Aboriginal Dreaming, The Eternal Prophet, Braxism, Confucianism, Taoism, Buddhism, Shenism, Judaism, Christianity, Sunni Islam, Shi'a Islam, Sufism, Hinduism, Jainism, Animism, Shinto, The Elegant, and Voodoo . . . . The list seemed endless.

As a result, Artama had the vocabulary to discuss the countless notions of the origin of life and the path to ultimate fulfillment . . . enlightenment . . . everlasting life.

+++++

One night, while Artama and Kora were discussing the cosmos, a glint of light came from the strings of the meteoron hanging on the wall. Kora noted this, stopped speaking, stood, set her chair away from the table, walked to the instrument, took it, walked back to the chair, seated herself gracefully, and began to play. The music resonated and reverberated.

Kora began to sing. Her voice was exquisitely, unnervingly beautiful.

Artama could barely breathe.

When she finished her song, Kora said, "I will teach you to play."

And they played, sang, and talked into the night.

In time, Kora said, with some trepidation in her voice, "*Your* time has come."

"I hope so."

"Eventually, you may think otherwise. This is merely preparation for many travails." Kora took Artama's hand. "Walk with me. Walk with me to my favorite place."

Kora's favorite place was a pool of the clearest water, surrounded by a low stone wall. The pool was perpetually filled by a spring: Water flowed over rocks, bubbles appeared and merged and burst . . . and the rocks, gradually . . . over vast time . . . had become rounded stones.

Artama wanted everything. He wanted to stay. He wanted to learn. He wanted to know

Kora. He wanted to see his father—his father must know. And The Readers—and the people—must know. He could feel the wound on his forehead healing.

+++++

In The Great Hall of The Academy of Anagnorisis, in the large antechamber of The Headmaster's office, Artama was seated in a high-backed upholstered chair, waiting in unsettled anticipation.

On a table were three globes, each with a different pattern of blue and green and tan and white, each held in a dark wooden stand carved with the fire of dragons.

An imposing door opened, and a tall man in an official black robe beckoned, "Headmaster Thorne welcomes you."

Seated before The Headmaster, Artama asked, "What are the three spheres?"

"Models. Our world—we refer to it as E1. Another world we call E2. And your world—E3.

"Enjoy your time here, Artama. You will long for these days."

+++++

Artama wanted the skill to defeat brutish ignorance on its own terms.

+++++

He studied under Antag, The Academy Master of Swordsmanship.

+++++

Artama knew he must return, enlighten the people, and comfort his father. But he longed to stay with Kora. Artama was now faced with *the* decision.   Thousands and thousands and thousands of books. Billions and billions and trillions of stars. A googol and a googol again. Unto a googolplexian. One choice to make.

+++++

Artama requested to speak again with The Headmaster.

Thorne poured water for Artama and gave him a cup. "Good afternoon. What is on your mind?"

"I want to return. I want to return to The Town . . . my people . . . and help."

Silence.

"And I want to stay with Kora."

"Of course, we knew this time would come." Thorne smiled. "It is your destiny."

"It is breaking my heart," Artama confessed.

"You will find your world brutish. Some will think you are an angel . . . even a god. Some will think you are a demon . . . even a devil."

Thorne stood and walked to a display of swords and reached for a simple hilt. He whirled the sword above his head and then pointed it toward the floor. There was no visible blade. Yet, the air was distorted as the blade passed through it, like the shimmering air in the heat of The Plain. Thorne walked toward Artama. "This invisible blade will be useful. I give you *The Crystal.*"

Artama shivered. He was floating in the middle of infinity . . . in the center of eternity. Solemnly he asked, "What is breaking my heart?"

"Love."

+++++

Artama knew he was seeing everything for the last time.

At the pool, Kora gave him a pack of items for his return: chocolate, a nutshell containing the amber ointment (the ointment that brought sight to his father), a small jar of the golden ointment (the ointment that healed his forehead and created the radiant star), a candle, and a needlebox. And Kora gave Artama the meteoron.

They sang to one another as the gold of the sun deepened and the purple clouds stretched across the sky.

They swam naked in the pool.

Lost in Kora's eyes, Artama saw his earth orbiting his sun, and he saw the dragon moon orbiting his earth. Artama saw clearly . . . eternally . . . infinitely . . . now.

Another split cocoon trembled, and ever so slowly, a glorious golden butterfly emerged. One by one, the cocoons opened, and as night fell, the weebon trees glowed in the aura of the metamorphoses. The golden butterflies lifted, swimming apparently erratically into the night.

+++++

On The Plain, Artama struggled through heat by day and cold by night. Beneath uncountable stars, the silence was profound.

+++++

At the Two Towers, there was a howling storm—as fierce as an unforgiving hurricane—a mountainous wall of dust.

+++++

Eventually, Artama encountered the bandits.

After some unpleasant banter, one of the outlaws drew his sword.

Artama sighed. He drew The Crystal from the scabbard on his back. The bandits saw only a hilt, not even a dagger, and they laughed. And then, they attacked, slashing viciously. Artama spun, parrying, warding off their assault. There was a fury of rapid cracking sounds and a flurry of bright flashes. The horses ran. The attackers were quickly disarmed, their swords knocked away into the dust. But not before Artama was wounded. Abandoning their swords, the thieves retreated to where the horses had stopped. They mounted and rode away cursing.

That night, with his fingertip, Artama applied a dab of the golden ointment to the cut on his shoulder and gently smoothed it over the wound.

+++++

At last, Artama saw The Town.

It was now enclosed by a wall.

As Artama approached the gate—from a parapet—one of the Kingsmen commanded, "Halt!"

"I am Artama, and I have returned!"

Artama was presumed dead, and only after a considerable debate, was he allowed to enter. A Kingsman sent for his father—someone who could identify him positively.

A crowd began to gather.

Eventually, Alagon arrived.

He took several unsteady steps forward and squinted at the tattered young man covered with the dust of The Plain.

A Kingsman demanded, "Well?"

The old man turned his back to the guard, faced the people, and proclaimed jubilantly, "My son has returned! My son is alive!"

Artama ran to his father, and father and son embraced.

A boy at the front of the crowd turned and ran toward his home in the heart of The Town, shouting, "Artama has returned! Artama is back from the dead!"

An old woman, sweeping in front of the doorway of her cottage, heard the boy as he ran past. Carrying her broom, she hurried inside, calling to her husband, "Artama is risen! Artama is risen from the dead!"

Alagon held Artama by the shoulders and looked deeply into his eyes. He leaned forward and whispered, "Beware, my son. These are dark times."

ARTAMA
& THE NEW KINGDOM

The Third Journey

***A NEW SINGULARITY**. A new moment of creation. Another beginning. Miraculous power without measure. No brilliance. No color. For light does not exist. Manifesting in absolute silence.*

Unobserved.

The unimaginable heat cools into gravity. Matter emerges as electrons and quarks. Antimatter appears. The strong force. The electroweak force becomes the electromagnetic and weak forces. Quarks form protons and neutrons. Antiquarks form antiprotons. Protons and antiprotons collide, creating photons.

Light.

Helium, lithium, and hydrogen . . . .

Atoms swirl into galaxies and coalesce into stars . . . or stars gather and form galaxies.

1

D'ANOR, the new King of kings, declared his reign by divine right—and by the might of the sword. Nam, the new God of gods, had anointed D'anor—so the people were told—and The Kingsmen honored The King and enforced his will.

The Town—now surrounded by a wall the height of five men—was renamed Eastedge.

There were constant rumors of war and endless tales of advancing marauders.

Arbitrary brutality was common. This was—after all—planet E3.

The Kingsmen were uniformed in black, and to protect themselves from the sun—or the chill of the night—they wore long, blood-red cloaks with hoods, capotes. Their scabbards held wicked blades. The Kingsmen manned the battlements, and they patrolled within the wall as well. Always watching.

By the grace of D'anor.

Inside the wall, directly across from the main gate, across an area of hard-packed dust, was the headquarters of The Kingsmen. Here, the soldiers reported for duty. When they could, they lingered and watched for attractive, young women walking to and from the market. Now, there was a small group of recruits dallying, waiting for orders.

"There's an ugly one for *you*," said a young private to a comrade.

The soldier responded, "Not for me, thank you. Maybe for *you*. If she'd have you, but I doubt it. Better yet, how about that old, skinny one in the brown dress?" He pointed to a white-haired, bent woman coming from the market, carrying a dirty, cloth sack.

The private pushed his comrade and laughed. "She looks more your age, graybeard."

The door of the headquarters opened, and an officer emerged.

One of The Kingsmen shouted, and the soldiers stopped their banter and came to attention, facing the headquarters.

Standing in the doorway, the officer presented a dashing image—tall, his red capote open, draping from his broad shoulders as a cape. Tribb was handsome—dark from the sun, with penetrating dark eyes. He was young for his rank. He was ambitious. "At ease!" he commanded.

The soldiers assumed the stance, legs apart, hands behind their backs at the waist.

Looking beyond them to his left, Tribb saw Cressa walking toward the market. To the soldiers, he ordered, "To your posts! Dismissed!"

The Kingsmen hurried away.

When the private saw Cressa, he stopped abruptly, and the graybeard collided with him.

The private said, "Look at that!"

The graybeard grumbled, "Keep moving." More quietly, he added, "And be careful. Tribb fancies her."

Cressa was a lovely girl with a radiant smile. Her teeth were as bright as stars in the night, and her hair was flowing black silk. Cressa was slender—yet becoming a woman. Exuberant with the love of life, her eyes were glimpses into wonder. Whenever she walked to the market, she hoped to see Tribb, and, almost childishly, quite foolishly, she had begun to flirt with him.

Their eyes met.

Cressa twirled, swinging her empty basket, her skirt rising some with her spin.

+++++

The circus was coming to Eastedge.

Every year since the wall was built, D'anor commissioned an extravaganza—a distraction.

When Artama had returned from across The Plain the first time, when he had returned from E1, although only a boy, he was received as a wonder. The Lord Most Honorable High Reader had declared that Artama should be The Writer and should write in *The Book of Knowledge & Wisdom*. As young as he was, Artama had taken his task seriously. Unfortunately, the tales of his journey had been twisted into stories of the discovery of gold and profane wealth, rather than enlightenment. Eventually, this led to the arrival of Zortan and his beastly horde. Zortan threatened to destroy The Town unless Artama led him across The Plain. Although not yet a young man, to save The Town, Artama agreed, knowing he could only lead the horde *onto* The Plain—*crossing* is a matter of the heart.

During Artama's absence, D'anor had established his rule, promising protection from marauders such as Zortan.

Now, preparations for the circus occupied everyone. The bakers were busily baking sweet treats. The aromas were intoxicating. Wagons laden with barrels of weebon wine were arriving at the public-house.

Weebon wine was made from the ripe, red fruit of the weebon tree. Although the trees grew throughout the kingdom, the only place they truly flourished was on the eastern slopes of the mountains near The Capital, near The Dragon Mountain and The Forest of Fire.

Beyond the wall around Eastedge, to the west, near the bend in the river, tents were being erected for lodging the performers and competitors—and the young women who traveled with the circus. The tents for the young women served a dual purpose. The raising of the tents was always a raucous time, with men shouting oaths and straining to set the poles and lift the canvas. Unlike the colorful tents for the circus itself—for the sideshows and vendors—the lodging tents were a drab, muddy brown. Although as dingy as any other, the tents for the young women would be easy to find, with red lanterns hanging above each entry.

Vendors from The Capital were already selling all manner of goods, from circus souvenirs to yarn and fabrics.

The new money changed hands constantly.

By the grace of D'anor.

+++++

There was another young man in Eastedge—not handsome, not an officer—a common man known as Korbin. His eyes were bright with zeal for his cause—the hope that Artama would lead a revolt against D'anor. Artama, who had led Zortan and his horde to destruction by dragons, who had twice crossed The Plain and returned, was now a young man of astonishing physical strength, prowess, and wisdom. Korbin was not physically strong, but his passion for justice was fierce, and he was tireless in his efforts to persuade Artama. Still, Artama insisted that revolution was not his mission.

At the base of the wall near the entrance to the market, Korbin knelt in the dust and drew a circle—the first element of the symbol of The Hope of The Radiant Star—the secret society of those who did not believe in Nam, who did not honor D'anor, who hoped Artama would change his mind.

+++++

Far away, on the western side of the mountains beyond The Capital, dark clouds were gathering.

+++++

It was the first day of the circus. Red and yellow tents glowed in the heat of the afternoon sun, and red and black pennants snapped in the desultory breeze. Jugglers on stilts strolled among the milling people. Crowds gathered around beguiling performers. The sword-swallowing woman tilted her head back, sliding a blade into her mouth, down her throat, all the way to the hilt. The mere sight of the dragon-man, with long red hair and skin like a reptile, frightened the children. Magicians held adults spellbound with triumphs of legerdemain. Acrobats performed incredible feats of balance and agility. Relentless competitors ran races. Vicious boxing and wrestling matches roused shouts and cheers. Clowns with painted white faces and grotesquely painted red smiles mocked everything.

In the open area inside the main gate, the children were gathered for a puppet show. Two puppet clowns were hitting each other with little loaves of bread, and the children were laughing.

Cressa, wearing a dark blue dress, was walking to market.

Tribb, in his black uniform and red capote, appeared from the headquarters, strode to her, and fell in step.

Cressa smiled and blushed.

"You are not at the circus," Tribb said.

"My mother will not allow it."

Tribb winked and turned away, walking back toward headquarters. Over his shoulder, he called, "Do you always do as your mother says?"

"Most of the time." Cressa's heart was throbbing.

+++++

While Artama was across The Plain, during his sojourn on E1, The Kingsmen assured the people D'anor would protect them.

By The King's decree, a wall was to be built.

With the new money—and the labor of the people—it came to pass.

Through multiple seasons, many worked at the river, digging the clay from the riverbank, and many worked making bricks— uncountable bricks. Others worked as masons, while others cared for the needs of those who labored.

The new money was spent freely by The Kingsmen, with the promise that d'anors could be exchanged for gold.

In time, the wall was built with battlements: parapets, crenels, and merlons. Thus, The Town, being the easternmost community of the realm, became Eastedge.

Most people rejoiced in the apparent new security and prosperity.

And The Kingsmen watched from the towers.

By the grace of D'anor.

+++++

Far away, on the east side of the mountains to the northwest, it began to rain—a thundering storm.

+++++

The Readings from *The Book of Knowledge & Wisdom*—events that once confirmed the community—were banned. The Readers were forbidden their robes, and Artama was forbidden from writing.

The Hall—where the people once gathered for The Readings—was maintained by D'anor merely as a museum of an unenlightened era. Now, whenever meetings were held, *The Book of Knowledge & Wisdom* was displayed behind the table of the elders as a relic of ignorance. The meetings were perfunctory, and a Kingsman was always present. Not many people came anymore, but there were some who sincerely—although foolishly—offered suggestions to be taken to D'anor.

Valdar, the former Lord Most Honorable High Reader, the former Reader in gold, was still regarded as the foremost citizen of Eastedge—except for Artama. The former Reader in black, the former Reader in white, and Artama's father were also held in high esteem.

Secretly, many people continued to refer to the elders as The Readers, but many wanted to abandon the old ways and embrace the new—the ways of D'anor. Many did not believe in anything. They merely held their silence and labored to avoid notice or trouble.

The Kingsman who observed the meetings in The Hall was usually Tribb. He enjoyed the chilling, intimidating effect he had on the proceedings. He memorized faces and names, and he enjoyed observing how carefully people chose their words in his presence.

The former Reader in white, Abrok, would dutifully record notes and chronicle the proceedings. Afterward, he would draft a register of requests to be presented to The King.

In time, some of the insignificant supplications were honored.

Significant pleas were ignored.

+++++

The new money was unlike the old money. It was not gold—or metal of any kind. It was more like lapa. The people were told d'anors were more convenient than gold: lighter, easier to carry—one bill representing many coins. The d'anor was The King's receipt: Anyone who wished to exchange d'anors for gold could do so—one fleck of gold for one d'anor. The King executed an effective shell game, moving gold from one region to satisfy the claims of another.

In time, the people viewed the currency to be as good as gold. It was money, and everyone accepted it.

Eventually, by edict of D'anor, for security, all gold was to be held in The King's treasury. The personal holding of gold was illegal, an act against the common good, an act against The King, and—ultimately—an act against Nam.

+++++

It was the second day of the circus. There were rows and rows of caged animals, strange creatures never before seen by the people of Eastedge. There were reptilian creatures, beasts looking like monsters from a tale of dragons. They had no wings or fire torching from their mouths, but they caused shudders among the crowd, nonetheless.

In a large cage, a tall, dark man in a golden costume commanded performing lions and tigers. At his behest, the cats would stand on their hind legs and dance. Just inside the cage was a basket for the collection of money, and the performer would banter with the spectators, cajoling them to fill it with d'anors, boasting that when it was overflowing, he would put his head into a lion's mouth. The basket filled often, and time and time again, he was faithful to his promise.

Vendors selling trinkets moved among the people, and the new money changed hands freely.

Although nothing was cheap.

At the base of the wall, Korbin crouched by the circle he had drawn in the dust the day before. He drew a line horizontally across it, extending beyond the circumference, representing two rays of light—two rays of hope.

Wherever the circus traveled, charlatans traveled as well. A fat clown—with a painted smiling face—worked with three nutshells and a pea. He was a wizard who could win or lose at will, and he could be wealthy—if he did not squander his money contemptuously on wine, food, and women.

He knew d'anors were nothing but tree bark.

Cressa stood near the back of the crowd watching the puppet show—a play about a fair maiden threatened by a fierce dragon with a long red tongue thrusting malevolently from its mouth. The dragon had skin of green sequins and a long, spiked tail. The fair maiden was calling for help in the comical voice of a man pretending to be a girl. The children stared with wide eyes and open mouths. Suddenly, bursting onto the scene was a puppet Kingsman brandishing a sword. The children cheered. The fair maiden hid behind him, peeking around him, first from one side and then the other. The dragon advanced, shaking its head, the red tongue flapping wildly.

"Hello," Tribb said, surprising Cressa.

She staggered into him. "You startled me."

Tribb steadied her, his thumb rubbing lightly against her breast.

The puppet Kingsman attacked the dragon, and there was a fierce battle—flailing red tongue and slashing sword.

The children shrieked with delight.

Tribb whispered to Cressa, and she glowed.

The dragon roared.

The maiden screamed.

The children shrieked all the more.

And again, Tribb whispered to Cressa—his arm still firmly around her.

The battle raged on until, at last, the puppet Kingsman jammed his sword into the dragon.

Cressa whispered to Tribb.

The dragon melodramatically swayed to and fro and finally slumped over the front edge of the showcase. The fair maiden ran to the puppet Kingsman.

The children cheered.

Tribb said loud enough for Cressa to hear above the noise, "On the final day of the circus, when the champions are being crowned, meet me beyond the last lodging tent, the one closest to the river." Then he walked off toward headquarters as though nothing had ever happened—no fair maiden in distress, no battle, no conversation.

+++++

The river was rising rapidly.

+++++

Nam was a wrathful god, the ultimate warlord who rewarded fealty with treasure. The priests portrayed him as a massive, majestic sovereign—with flowing black hair and beard, with massive shoulders and arms, a deep chest, and legs as stout as stone pillars. His gold crown was a spiked helmet. There was no kindness in his eyes, only a ferocious blaze. He towered above mortal men and brandished a broadsword against all infidels. He had no tolerance for wavering allegiance. Those who obeyed His commands would be rewarded with eternal life in His Kingdom beyond the grave. Food would be a never-ending, sumptuous feast. Wine glasses would be forever overflowing. Those who did not obey would burn in the smelting fires, purifying the gold of His everlasting reign.

It was the third day of the circus.

In the late-afternoon golden light, outside the public-house, to a crowd of revelers, a minstrel sang songs of adventure, most about Artama. The heat of the day was fading into comfort, and the roisterers—drowning their hangovers from yesterday—drank and laughed and spilled their weebon wine.

Near the base of the wall, Korbin crouched by his drawing in the dust and completed the symbol, adding a second line, vertically: two more rays of hope. His drawing was an artistic abstraction, an elemental representation of the star that glowed on Artama's forehead. The star was something venerated. The drawing was a message in the dust.

Korbin stood and walked toward the market. A woman in a long dress, wearing a shawl about her head and shoulders, who had been tarrying nearby, covertly watching him, taking far too long to select her squash and beans, immediately turned away from the produce stand and walked to the drawing in the dust. Seeing the completed symbol, she understood the message she was to begin circulating, and she hurried away.

+++++

In the evening, as the red sky was darkening, there was a gathering of those who had been notified—a secret meeting of The Hope of the Radiant Star. Far from the gate and the crowds of the circus, a small congregation was assembled in one room of a simple home.

Korbin stood before the group, speaking passionately.

The former Reader in black, Hape, sat at the back of the room, near the door, listening. Back in the time of The Town, when The Readers read from *The Book of Knowledge & Wisdom*, Hape was The Honorable Second Reader. Unlike the other Readers—who were in awe of young Artama when he returned from across The Plain the first time—Hape resented the boy for challenging the authority of *The Book*, and thereby the stature of The Readers, and that resentment lingered—a constantly rankling, gnawing obsession. The room was hot, and he wiped his brow with a handkerchief.

Korbin proclaimed, "We *must* convince him. He is the only one who can unite the realms."

"But *how*? How do we persuade him?" asked a young man seated near the front of the group.

"Why try?" challenged an old man. "It would be futile. We have no weapons—no army to lead. What is he to do? Confronting The Kingsmen would be suicide."

"Better to resist and die than grovel and live," the young man replied.

A young woman in a well-worn dress stood, and everyone turned toward her. "Many times, he has told us the sword is not the solution."

"What *is* the solution?" the young man demanded.

She calmly replied, "He speaks of higher things—matters of the heart, matters of the soul."

An old woman stood, waving her arms above her head, shouting, "He speaks of other worlds! And someplace he calls E1—wherever *that* is. Frankly, I am tired of it. *He* caused Zortan to threaten us. *He* caused the rise of D'anor. What good is there in having him among us? *He* is the root of our plight."

Korbin replied, "Or is he the answer to our prayers?"

There was a knock at the door. Hape acted quickly—checking through the peephole, unlocking the door, and letting in the messenger. Urgently, Hape closed the door. The messenger was a young man with anxious eyes. Barely audibly, he told Hape, "The ceremonies at the circus are concluding."

Hape signaled to Korbin and left immediately, walking quickly away from the residential area toward the circus, toward the public-house.

The messenger was the next to exit, walking away in the opposite direction.

Without a conclusion to the debate, the meeting ended abruptly. Quickly, individually, each person left, walking into the impending darkness.

Korbin was the last to leave.

+++++

By now, the public-house was crowded beyond capacity with spectators from the circus. Merrymakers were milling around in front of the building, drinking, talking about the marvels they had witnessed. The fat clown was working near the right front corner of the building, and drunken men were making side bets on those who thought they could outwit him.

At the left front corner of the building, at the edge of the crowd, unnoticed by the revelers, Hape and Tribb were engaged in conversation.

Inside the building, the barroom was hot, with drunken men jostling one another. Serving wenches pushed through the crowd, and rude comments were made by both men and women, but the mood was festive. Seated at the end of the bar were two traveling merchants who had left the circus early to get the best seats. They were talking with each other and the barmaid—whenever she came their way. The older of the two men traded in weebon wine, and the younger in baubles and beads. Business was good, and they were both in high spirits. The barmaid came to them and leaned forward, resting her elbows on the bar. The two men were delighted. Perspiration glistened at her cleavage. She managed a smile and wiped her face with a wet bar towel. The wine merchant said, "A priest, a stableboy, and a Kingsman walked into a bar—"

And the barmaid said, "Holy shit, there's going to be trouble."

Both men laughed, and the older said, "A bright one she is." He turned to his companion and added, "Young man, buy her a drink."

"*You* buy her a drink. *You* are the wine vendor."

The barmaid announced, "*One* of you buy me a drink. I'll come back when you decide." She turned and began talking with other customers.

Outside, Hape and Tribb finished their conversation and nonchalantly walked away in different directions.

+++++

After his second return from across The Plain, Artama, only a young man, was virtually imprisoned by his fame. Often, he wrapped his brow with a scarf—a bandana—to conceal the golden glow of The Radiant Star in the center of his forehead.

But everyone knew the tale, and people came from every realm to talk with him, seeking his advice.

A vexation to D'anor.

+++++

It was almost dark, and Korbin was nearly home when three Kingsmen on horseback stopped him, forming a triangle around him. Facing him was Tribb, astride a black destrier. To the left, on a mahogany bay, was a young Kingsman with a hesitant look in his eyes. To the right, on a blood bay, was a veteran Kingsman. His eyes were apathetic, cold.

Tribb demanded, "Where have you been?"

Korbin felt heat blaze up his spine to the base of his skull. The heat spread across his shoulders, and his forehead beaded with perspiration. He envisioned an explosion of light, and then, the flash was replaced with the incandescent red of a heated iron rod. He managed to respond to Tribb, saying, "What is this? What is this about?"

But he knew.

Tribb said, "Where have you been?"

A few people who were returning from the circus stopped to watch. Most looked away and continued walking.

Tribb glared at those who tarried and put his hand to the hilt of his sword. "Move on!"

The people scurried away.

Tribb turned back to his men and commanded, "Take him!"

The Kingsmen dismounted. Korbin turned to face the young soldier to his left, and the other knocked him to the ground with one blow of his cudgel. Tribb glared at the hesitant Kingsman, and, after a moment, the young soldier kicked Korbin in the back, at his kidneys, twice. The older Kingsman kicked Korbin in the stomach several times, and then, as Korbin struggled to breathe, the younger soldier kicked him in the face and laughed.

As Korbin lay unconscious on the ground, they gagged him and bound him. Then, they threw him over the back of Tribb's horse.

With their prisoner, The Kingsmen rode away.

By the command of Tribb, the decree of D'anor, and the will of Nam.

For Korbin, the worst was yet to come. Disappearances were not uncommon, and unknown consequences were more terrifying than certain knowledge. Even on E3, people knew some fates were worse than death.

+++++

In her cottage, in the comfort of her bed, listening to the wind, in anticipation of tomorrow evening, Cressa could not sleep. Lying on her back, she smiled at the ceiling. She envisioned walking with Tribb along the river, holding hands as the golden setting sun began turning red. She rolled onto her left side and lay looking out the open window. After the heat of the day, the night air was pleasantly cool and fresh. She pushed her hands under her pillow, raising her head a little, and took several deep breaths. Faintly, she heard music and laughter from somewhere. She visualized laughing with Tribb as they held hands, listening to the music. She imagined they kissed. Cressa was in no hurry to sleep—she was enjoying her fantasy.

Nonetheless, eventually, she drifted into dreams—unpleasant, disturbing visions. Tribb stepped toward her—holding a red scarf stretched between his hands. Cressa backed away and shivered.

+++++

Eastedge was parched, but the river was overflowing—raging.

LIGHT, _electromagnetic radiation, propagates as waves, yet the energy of the waves is absorbed in distinct locations as particles. The absorbed energy is the quanta of light—photons. When a wave is transformed and absorbed as a photon, the energy of the wave instantly collapses to a single location—the wavefunction collapse—exhibiting the dual, wave-like and particle-like, nature of light, the wave-particle duality._

Light exerts physical pressure on objects—photons strike and transfer their momentum, yet, upon being released, they instantaneously proceed at light speed.

2

IT WAS THE FINAL DAY of the circus.

The sun was new to the sky, and the air was cool. Already people were heading for the rings to secure the best views. The baker's children were peddling circus dreams—small butter cakes drenched with frosting. The proprietor of the public-house was prospering as well, selling wee-cho—the hot drink brewed from the roasted seeds of the weebon. Youngsters were looking for friends. Adolescents were flirting.

Today was the final day of competition. In the evening, the champions would be crowned and prizes would be awarded— medallions hanging from ribbons and, most importantly, d'anors. For the competitors— and the flirting teens—there were only last chances now.

Among the throng, there were, here and there, small groups gathered, people not in a festive mood, people who were discussing Korbin and the event of last night. There were few facts but many speculations. A small number who had seen the incident were quietly telling what they knew—some in angry voices, others sadly.

In one group, a gray-haired man with a cane was saying, "I stood out of sight and peered around the corner of a cottage. They beat him into unconsciousness."

"You did nothing?" asked a young woman.

"And what was I to do?" the man growled, stabbing his cane into the dust, "Attack three Kingsmen armed with swords?"

"Then what?" asked a young man.

"They threw him over a horse and rode off."

An old woman said, "I doubt we ever see him again."

The others lowered their heads and looked at the dust at their feet.

+++++

Cressa was home, thinking about Tribb. She imagined herself in the golden light of the westering sun, walking with him, or riding with him on his great stallion. Her heart was fluttering.

Cressa had not yet seen the river in its swollen rage.

+++++

Tribb was walking atop the wall, thinking about The King. How could he most benefit from his knowledge? Korbin was valuable, but Tribb's relationship with Hape could bring a career in The Capital, away from the damnable dust of The Plain.

If he could only bring Artama down.

Tribb imagined himself in The Palace, in a splendidly imposing uniform, eating fine food and drinking wine from a golden goblet.

Officers saluted him.

Beautiful women were at his command.

Northwest of The Capital, beyond the river, the raw grandeur of the mountains was intimidating, humbling. The eastern slopes were covered in the vivid red of The Forest of Fire. The peaks rose into the luminous sky. The rain had stopped, and the brilliance of the blue was overwhelming. The sun was almost white.

The river was rampaging southeast toward the eastern edge of The Kingdom.

The Capital was much larger than Eastedge and surrounded by a wall as well. The wall formed a square, encompassing a vast area of cottages and commerce. In the center of the square was The Palace, encircled by another wall. Outside the circle was a moat, fed by a channel from the river, the inflow and outflow controlled by gates. Inside The Palace wall, the grounds were irrigated and verdant. Exotic flowering plants bloomed in brilliant red and yellow and blue.

The Palace was a fortress, the exterior austere.

The interior was an orgy of gold.

The Council Chamber was not large, but it was splendid. The walls were paneled in wood from far beyond The Kingdom, a wood known as Melting Gold. It had taken more than two years to transport the rough-cut timber from the forest where it grew. In all of The Kingdom, Melting Gold was only seen in The Council Chamber. The paneling was iridescent. The grain gave the appearance of rivulets of molten gold running down the walls. There were no windows in The Chamber. Lavish purple drapery hung behind The Throne. The Throne itself was huge, with an extravagantly carved back in the form of a sunburst glorified with gold leaf. The cushions of The Throne were deep and sumptuous, and they were the royal purple color of the drapery.

In The Chamber, arranged in an arc before The Throne, there were eight grand Chairs, where the members of The Council were seated, all awaiting the arrival of The King.

The Jester wore a black and white costume—the trousers black on the left leg and white on the right—the tunic white on the left and black on the right. His face was painted in black and white as well. Although his image portrayed stark contrasts, he deftly dealt in subtle shades of gray. He held his bauble, his scepter, firmly in his right hand. Although The Jester had no vote, he truly sat at the right hand of The King.

To The Jester's right sat The Commander General. His costume was an extravagantly military uniform: dark brown, with heavy medals covering the left side of his chest and colorful insignia on both sleeves from the shoulder to the elbow. Although beyond the age of combat, The Commander was a dominating physical presence—erect, muscular, forbidding.

To the right of The Commander General sat The High Priest. He was the oldest man in

The Chamber, with a long white beard and cynical eyes beneath luxuriant, unruly white eyebrows. He wore a hooded black robe—the hood pulled down over his forehead. The High Priest spoke for Nam—thus, he was invaluable to D'anor.

Continuing counter-clockwise around the arc of The Council, next was The Minister of The Treasury. His robe was emerald green. As he waited for the arrival of The King, he examined a freshly printed d'anor, holding it between his hands, turning it from front to back and back again. He was satisfied with the work.

Next to the Minister of The Treasury, there was a break in the arc of imposing chairs, a wide aisle leading from the main entrance of The Council Chamber to The Throne.

On the other side of the aisle, wearing a dark gray robe, The Minister of Commerce was seated, holding a large ledger in his lap. Trade had been especially brisk of late, meaning more taxes, and he was eager to report the numbers if given a chance.

In the next seat, in a yellow robe, was The Minister of Information. His responsibility was to gather intelligence and provide accurate information to The Council and The King.

Next, The Minister of Education, in his dark blue robe, was responsible for disseminating whatever propaganda The Council and The King deemed useful.

Completing the arc, in a Chair immediately to The King's left, wearing his crimson robe, was The Minister of Law. He could argue any point successfully, and, without fail, his arguments supported D'anor.

+++++

In Eastedge, in The Hall, in a small room behind the main chamber, the elders were seated at a table, talking quietly. The mood was grim. Hape was saying, "I have confirmed that Korbin was indeed arrested. He is to be taken to The Capital—and there to stand before The King—charged with treason and blasphemy.”

Abrok ran his fingers through his hair. “How did this come to pass?”

“Last night, I am told, on his way home from a gathering of The Hope of The Radiant Star, he was stopped and questioned.”

Valdar sighed. “We knew this day would come.”

Abrok nodded toward the wine cellar door. “Does Artama know?”

Valdar answered, “He does not. He has been downstairs writing all morning.”

Hape puffed his cheeks. “Tomorrow, I will ride before the circus caravan to The Capital. I will seek The King to plead on behalf of Korbin. I will carry Abrok’s register as well.”

“I am afraid it is futile,” said Abrok.

Valdar countered, “Hape, I pray for your success.”

Hape looked to the floor.

Valdar heard the river raging. With an unsettling, unforeseen sense of irony, he added, "Peace be with you."

+++++

Parting the purple drapery, stepping into The Chamber, wearing a purple robe and a crown of gold, D'anor appeared—wearing a golden mask. The mask was the exquisite work of the artisans beyond the mountains: a disarmingly handsome visage. Gold necklaces, heavy with gems, hung down his chest. Gold rings, set with more precious stones, adorned every finger.

The members of The Council stood—and in unison bowed.

D'anor strode to The Throne, the sound of his boot heels echoing from the Melting Gold, and seated himself.

Only then did the members of The Council take their seats.

The Jester, his black-on-white makeup portraying a grim countenance, cleared his throat, but he did not speak.

Unseen, D'anor winced as his mask rubbed against his infected face.

+++++

Artama's father, Alagon, was alone in the production shop—the large room added to the original cottage, providing space for the apprentices to work. But on this day, the apprentices were at the circus, and no work would be done.

Artama was away as well—writing.

Normally, the shop was busy. Artama and his father supervised the production of the pottery, and the demand was great. It seemed everyone wanted something from Artama. Some admired the artful, abstract designs, while others valued the unique colors and superior glazes. Most simply wanted something touched by the hand of the one who had crossed The Plain and returned. Anything Artama touched was treasured. A few people paid in d'anors, but most would trade. Highly prized was lapa, the sheets upon which Artama wrote. (Thin strips of the pith of the lapa plant were soaked, laid together, pressed, and dried. Those who lived near the lakes where the plant grew, made it. This was illegal, but remote areas were rarely patrolled by The Kingsmen. Lapa was easy to transport—rolled in a blanket, or carried across the back, hidden beneath a tunic or a cloak.) On these sheets, Artama was desperately trying to record the knowledge from E1—his never-ending impossible task.

Also highly valued were plants Artama could use in making medicines. It seemed Artama could work miracles, and many people came to be cured.

Others simply, reverently, brought gifts.

Now, in solitude, Alagon had moved to the reading table.

He was thinking about life.

He was very old, yet, still, he missed his wife. She had died when Artama was only a boy. Alagon was both old and alone. Artama was his pride, but Artama was claimed by the people and taken by his destiny.

The old man looked at his shaking hands. He stood and steadied himself with one hand on the table, the table where Artama used to sit and read to him—when Alagon was blind. Together, they shared the beauty and the wisdom of the literature. Now, Alagon walked to the workbench, where, until recently, he had painted patterns on the pottery Artama made. He took a brush, dipped it in a pot of red, intending to decorate a plate. His hand trembled. He made a stroke. He tried another. And another. Heavily, he sighed in acceptance—he could no longer execute his intentions.

He knew his end was near.

+++++

In The Council Chamber, D'anor adjusted his mask and demanded, "What news?"

The Minister of Information was the first to speak. "My Lord, Artama continues to be a vexation—if not a curse. There is increasing talk of a growing secret society of those who would follow him . . . against you. Reports of such citizens are coming from every realm."

D'anor hit the armrest of The Throne with his right fist. "Such *citizens* are not citizens! They are *traitors*!"

Shifting anxiously in his seat, The Minister of Information corrected himself, "Reports of such traitors are coming from every realm." He hesitated. "My Lord . . . more and more are claiming he is . . . holy . . . even resurrected."

"Blasphemy!" shouted The High Priest from across the aisle.

"If he is resurrected, I want to know his secret," gibed The Jester, as only he would dare.

The High Priest scowled.

D'anor raised his right hand. "Enough."

The Chamber was silent.

The Jester tapped his scepter on the floor.

D'anor spoke: "The question remains: What is to be done? At the advice of this esteemed Council, I have tolerated him, not wanting to arouse the people. Has the time come to take him?"

"Whatever you wish," said The Minister of Law.

"If I imprison him, his confinement will be a festering irritation to the people." The King flinched as the mask rubbed against a pustule on his cheek. "If I publicly execute him, the passions of the people will be set ablaze."

"And we will absolutely extinguish them," responded The Commander General.

The Minister of Information, craving to be of value, added, "I should also say, My Lord, it is reported that Artama is reluctant. He is not eager to lead an uprising. This is a complaint of many."

"Then let them squabble among themselves," suggested The Jester. "Be slow to take action that would make him a martyr."

The Minister of Education interjected, "And while the people are bickering, we could redouble our campaign to discredit him."

"We will have a better understanding after the circus returns from Eastedge," said The Minister of Information as he nodded to The Commander General. "Tribb will bring the latest news."

"Then we shall await the arrival of Tribb," concluded D'anor.

But The Minister of Commerce spoke: "My Lord, may I address another matter?"

"Speak."

"My Lord, we need more money spent in the western realm. The people are increasingly impatient about their circumstances."

"How much money?"

"Perhaps, two or three hundred d'anors per person."

The King looked to The Minister of The Treasury and commanded, "Make more d'anors . . . as necessary."

The King surveyed the arc of The Council. "Is there anything else?"

The Jester suggested, "Send the circus."

The King nodded to The Minister of Commerce. "Send the circus with the money."

Again, The King scanned The Council. "Anything else?"

The Chamber was silent.

"Then, we will meet again when Tribb arrives." D'anor stood.

The Council stood. In unison, the members bowed.

The King swept out of The Chamber.

+++++

The sun was lowering, and the circus crowd was in a full-throated roar. Tribb was riding leisurely toward the river, swinging wide behind the tents to avoid being noticed. He was wondering if Cressa would come.

And he was planning his meeting with The King.

+++++

Cressa had no looking-glass, but she knew she was blessed with beauty. Unnecessarily—for her beauty transcended adornment—she fixed a flower in her hair, uncertain about this evening.

As she was about to leave her cottage, her mother said, "Wait."

Cressa caught her breath.

"Let me look at you. Turn around for me."

Cressa spun around and faced her mother again.

"No, sweetheart . . . slowly."

Cressa slowly turned.

"You are surely pretty." Her mother stepped forward and adjusted a shoulder strap. "We need to make some new dresses for you. This is a little tight on top. You are becoming a woman."

Cressa blushed.

Her mother smiled. "All right, sweetheart, have fun. Enjoy the puppets." And then, she added, "Stay inside the wall, and be home by dark."

"Bye-bye, Mama."

As Cressa walked through town, her thoughts were swirling. She knew better. She wanted to meet Tribb, but she feared it was a mistake.

Cressa *knew* it was a mistake.

When she arrived at the puppet show, she stopped and watched from the back of the crowd. A boy she knew, Hadee, waved to her, and she waved back. The audience began to laugh at something in the show, and Cressa moved a little more around the back of the crowd, toward the gate. She was thinking about her mother, and she was thinking about Tribb. The audience roared with laughter. Cressa quickly joined the people walking out the gate.

She was outside.

The line had been crossed.

Cressa hurried along the wall, turning the corner and walking in the direction of the river.

Soon, she came to the tents of the performers, competitors, and harlots. Drunken men with wild, leering eyes were everywhere. She walked more quickly, still thinking about her mother. And thinking about Tribb.

One of the drunks shouted, "Hey, pretty girl, come here a minute!"

Another yelled, "Slow down, beautiful. Let us take a look!"

Cressa wanted to turn back. She hesitated, stopped walking.

"Come over here and have a little wine," called a gaunt man with several missing teeth. He was sitting at a table with three other men and two women. The men were playing jord, a dice game, gambling. The women—all in dresses with provocative necklines—were fawning over the men who were winning. The man with the missing teeth tilted his head back and drank from a wineskin, wine running down his chin. Then, obscenely, he pointed the spigot toward Cressa and squeezed. "We could use some pleasant company!" the man bellowed. "All these tarts want is our money."

Everyone laughed.

"That's not *all* we want," one of the women said, "but I think his wineskin is the best he has to offer."

Everyone laughed again.

Cressa started walking—toward the river.

"Hey, come back!" the man shouted.

"Leave her alone," said one of the women. "You have more than you can handle right here."

They all snickered.

Cressa heard the river. The sun was lowering in the sky, and the light was becoming golden. She remembered a time, as a child, walking with her mother along the river in the golden light of the late-afternoon sun. Her mother was holding her hand and humming a tune. Cressa would always remember the wonder of that day, and she would forever recall the melody.

She began humming.

The river was raging.

Cressa knew better than to disregard her mother. She knew better than to be meeting Tribb.

Beyond the tents, near the river, there were stacks of unused bricks (each stack taller than two men). Next to the stacks were heaps of discarded, broken bricks, remnants of the building of the wall.

Cressa slowed as she neared the stacks and heaps. She had never seen the river so high and wild. She had never heard such a sound. She stopped.

From behind a stack of bricks, in his black uniform and red capote, with a red scarf around his neck, Tribb appeared on a huge, black destrier.

There was a roar from the crowd at the circus.

"You came," said Tribb. He brought his horse closer and leaned over Cressa.

"I did," she said. "But I should get back."

"I will take you for a ride along the river."

"My mother will be looking for me."

"The sun is only beginning to set." Tribb reined his horse close to a heap of broken bricks. "Have you ever seen the river so powerful?"

"I should get back."

"Step up those bricks and climb up behind me."

Cressa hesitated.

Tribb extended his left arm and beckoned with his smile.

Looking into the darkness of his eyes, Cressa paused. She trembled—but she could not resist. Clasping his hand, she stepped up the bricks and swung up behind him, wrapping her arms around his waist, her left hand brushing against the hilt of his sword.

They loped off toward the edge of the river.

They rode against the current, just at the edge of the seething water, occasionally splashing in it. Cressa was thrilled. The sound was frightening. She squinted into the exhilarating, rushing air and golden sunlight. Tribb's red scarf blew in her face.

In time, Tribb reined the horse around, and at a deliberate pace, they rode with the current.

Cressa absorbed the warmth of the sun on her back . . . the warmth of Tribb as she held him . . . and the warmth of the horse beneath her.

Tribb was thinking about D'anor, Korbin, Hape, and the whores in the tents.

Cressa knew she was betraying her mother's trust.

At last, Tribb brought the horse to a stop at the bricks. "Hop off."

Cressa climbed down onto a heap and stepped down to the dust.

Tribb dismounted and said, "Now, was that fun?"

"Oh, yes!"

Tribb advanced and smiled. He reached out and took her by the hands.

Cressa stiffened.

Tribb laughed. "What?"

"I should get back."

"So soon?"

"My mother will be expecting me."

"Where did you tell her you were going?"

"To the puppet show."

"You did not mention us?"

"No." Cressa was frightened.

"I have a gift for you," Tribb said, untying his scarf and holding it out.

"No. Please. You do not need to. I could not take it home."

"But I want to."

Tribb held the scarf between both hands and stepped toward Cressa.

She backed away and shivered.

"You are cold?" Tribb advanced again. "If you cannot keep it, then just wear it for a while. Let me put it across your shoulders." He moved behind her.

Cressa stood motionless, but her mind was churning.

In an instant, the scarf was across her mouth—a red gag drawn tight, biting into the corners of her mouth. Next, she was face down in the dust with the scarf knotted tightly at the back of her head. She was choking in the dust. She knew she was ruined. Her head was yanked back, and Tribb's dagger was at her throat. She tried to scream—in vain—and then she began to sob.

"Shut up!"

Cressa was totally alone. She remembered walking with her mother along the river in the golden light of the late-afternoon sun, her mother holding her hand and humming a tune. She wanted to apologize to her mother and beg forgiveness, but she knew she would die with the words unspoken.

"If you ever speak a word of this to anyone, I will kill you!" Tribb pressed the dagger to her throat with his right hand. "Do you understand me?" With his left hand, he raised her skirt.

Cressa sobbed.

"I said shut up! You are nothing but a peasant girl. *I* am a Kingsman. I can do what I want. When I am finished with you, I think I *will* kill you—you teasing bitch—and throw your body in the river."

Laughter. Loud, drunken laughter. A group of men and women from the tents came around the corner of the heaps and stacks, passing a flagon among them. When they saw The Kingsman, they stopped.

Tribb got to his feet.

Instantly, Cressa was up and running, struggling with the knot in the scarf as she ran.

Tribb glared at the group of drunks.

They slowly backed away.

Tribb mounted his horse and galloped off, following the edge of the river upstream, furiously.

Cressa pulled off the scarf and threw it.

And ran and ran and ran.

TIME: *a verisimilitude, a biological construct.*

Often apprehended as an interval or a series of intervals. In some realms, the intervals are defined by the distance light travels. Space-time: a light-second, a light-minute, a light-year . . . .

Amid the constancy of the speed of light and the relativity of the perception of time, time stops at the speed of light.

Moments are simultaneously eternal.

There is only now.

3

THE NEXT DAY, by midday, the circus wagons were rolling northwest to The Capital. Hape and Tribb rode at the front of the caravan. Immediately behind them was the prisoner's wagon, a black box drawn by two black horses reined by a Kingsman. In the door at the back of the black box, and on each side, was a window with bars. On the outside of each window, a red curtain was drawn closed.

Inside the box was Korbin.

Hape knew he had information valuable to The King. He knew Artama knew secrets—secrets that could make D'anor truly seem a god. If he cleverly and gradually revealed his knowledge, Hape believed he would win favor with D'anor—perhaps even be honored with a seat in The Council. Hape had no intention of troubling The King with the register of requests Abrok had prepared.

Tribb knew The King would value Korbin and Hape: Korbin was the leader of The Hope of The Radiant Star, and Hape knew the secret thoughts and actions of Artama (and the other former Readers—Artama's confidants). In return for arresting Korbin and introducing Hape, Tribb believed his aspirations would be secured. He saw himself commanding Kingsmen, imagined himself feasting at The King's table, and visualized himself in bed with two drunken girls.

Hape knew Tribb was not to be trusted.

Likewise, Tribb knew Hape.

The two maleficent riders talked as they rode, each adroitly concealing his true intentions.

Tribb fell back alongside the black box.

Hape fell back with him.

Tribb reined close to a side window and swept back the curtain. He peered into the box. Korbin was lying on his side, curled in filthy straw on the floor. His eyes opened, and Tribb closed the curtain.

The flash of light shocked the darkness and roused Korbin from his phantasmagoria, but as soon as he opened his eyes, the brightness was replaced with a glowing rectangle of red. With difficulty, he raised on an elbow. His wrists were shackled. There was another glowing rectangle beyond his feet. His ankles were shackled. To his left, another red glow. Korbin fell back into the repulsive straw. His head was aching, and his face was swollen. He touched the welts on his forehead and cheeks and felt dried blood. He tried to rise again, but there was a sharp pain in his side, and he fell back into the stench. His ribs hurt. Breathing was a struggle.

He heard voices and tried to focus and listen. The sounds were coming from outside, from where the light had momentarily exploded. Toward the window, he slowly crawled through the vile straw. He forced himself to sit up, and he leaned against the wall. Over the rattling of the wagon, it was difficult to understand what was being said, but he could apprehend a few words: The Capital . . . The King . . . The Council.

And now he recognized the voices: Tribb and Hape.

Hape, the despicable traitor!

All would be lost!

Korbin slumped to the floor and vomited. The pain in his ribs was excruciating. He rolled in the straw, his thoughts rampant with images of Kingsmen bursting into cottages and arresting fathers and mothers. Children were screaming and crying. He saw Valdar and Abrok knocked to the ground. Kingsmen kicked them and spat. Artama's father was dragged from his cottage. Artama himself was shackled, stripped naked, and paraded through Eastedge—through the market and past the headquarters of The Kingsmen. He was flogged until he collapsed. Then he was thrown into the back of a prisoner's wagon, and the wagon was driven out the main gate, surrounded by mounted Kingsmen . . . disappearing into the dust.

Korbin was lying face down in the straw.

Helpless.

How could he warn anyone?

What had he done?

What had he caused?

+++++

In a room of golden splendor, the largest room in The Palace, designed to accommodate grand celebrations—feasts and music and dancing—D'anor sat alone.

The banquet hall was rectangular. Running lengthwise along the wall opposite the entrance was The King's table, a table that could seat thirty on each side. The wall behind the banquet table was a wall of tall windows. Tonight, the heavy curtains were drawn closed to keep out the chill. In rows parallel to the King's table were tables for as many as two hundred guests. The space separating The King's banquet board and the tables of the quests was large enough for fifty couples to dance. When facing The King, in an area to the right of his table, there was a raised platform, a stage upon which musicians would play for the pleasure of revelers. Tonight, the hall was dark, except for six magnificent, golden candelabra on the King's table—three to the left and three to the right of D'anor. In the area directly in front of the table, there were eight torches in elaborate, golden stands. In addition, six similar torches illuminated the stage.

D'anor sat alone at the center of the table, facing an empty room. Although the hall was desolate, the banquet table was covered with plates and bowls of roasted meats and vegetables. The King wore his golden, feasting mask, a mask with the chin cut away, allowing him to indulge his appetite, although revealing an obscene, festering pustule.

A servant girl entered the hall, walked briskly to The King, and refilled his goblet with wine. He grabbed her wrist, drank the wine, and set his chalice on the table. He released

her, and she refilled the goblet. Then, she
scurried out. D'anor slurped more wine. He
tore a chunk from a loaf of bread and dipped it
in gravy. He bit into the bread, chewed
impatiently, and swallowed. He drank more
wine.

Four musicians, three with stringed
instruments and one with a flute, entered the
hall and took their positions on the small
stage. They settled themselves and began
tuning.

The tuning irritated D'anor. He wanted
music. "Play!" he commanded.

And the musicians began playing—a
bright melody, although slightly sour.

Tonight, D'anor was especially irritable.
The circus and Tribb were expected, and
D'anor was anxious for news from Eastedge.
The Artama dilemma was constantly annoying,
gnawing into his thoughts, spoiling his
pleasures.

Five dancing girls swirled into the room.
Selected and brought to The Palace from the

far reaches of The Kingdom and beyond—instructed in manners and methods—these were among the most pleasing of the current concubines. As they each twirled in a revolving circle in the torchlight, D'anor studied them, contemplating his choice for the night. The Negro girl caught his attention first. Such black beauty was rarely seen. The golden light of the torches glistened on her splendid, ebony flesh. Or would it be the blond girl? Golden hair and blue eyes were as rare as deep purple-black. The tallest girl, with slender yet powerful legs, was promisingly tempting. The full-breasted beauty bounced proudly. The girl with auburn hair and smoldering eyes was like smoke rising from the fire of lust.

+++++

Korbin was rousted from the prisoner's wagon and led haltingly across a muddy yard by two Kingsmen. Everyone was slipping in the mire. Korbin fell, and the soldiers laughed. "You pig!" shouted one of the guards. "Wallow, pig, wallow." Korbin was face down in the muck.

He rolled onto his back. The guards, cursing, lifted him to his feet and pushed him toward a locked door. One of the Kingsmen pounded on the door. Nothing. He pounded again. Eventually, the door was opened, and two other Kingsmen took charge, one on either side. They closed the door, and the two soldiers outside cautiously made their way back to the wagon. Inside, Korbin was pushed along. Leading the way was a third Kingsman, bearing a torch. He led them through a narrow corridor and down three flights of stairs to a large, dank chamber with cells along each wall. The floor was dirt. The Kingsman placed his torch in a rusted bracket on the wall. He removed a heavy ring of keys from his belt and opened an empty cell. Korbin was pushed inside and fell to the floor. One of the Kingsmen spat on him. The door was locked, the torch was removed from the bracket, and the three Kingsmen climbed the stairs, leaving the cells in total darkness. Korbin, covered with mud, lay with his face in the dirt—in the footprints and foulness of many before him. The pain of his broken ribs was suffocating. His mind roiled with visions of Kingsmen bursting into cottages, children screaming, and Artama being flogged bloodily into unconsciousness.

+++++

The music pulsed, and the concubines danced erotically, each one in turn—for a moment in time—moving alluringly toward The King. The black dancer smiled broadly, her bright, white teeth gleaming in starry contrast to her midnight skin. The blond was next. She stopped, bowed low, and then snapped her head back, creating a golden explosion of long, sun-bright hair. The tallest of the dancers moved close to the dining table, stopped, turned around, spread wide her long, powerful legs, bent forward, her head almost touching the floor, and smiled between her legs at D'anor. Next, it was the full-breasted beauty's turn. She stopped, removed her top, threw her arms out sideways, and inhaled deeply. The last of the dancers, the last to make her appeal, the smoldering girl with auburn hair, puckered her full lips and blew a kiss, setting D'anor on fire.

D'anor licked his greasy lips and drank more wine.

The courtesans whirled away, their golden bracelets and anklets chattering and gleaming.

Each paramour was told she had been selected specially to bring beauty to The King. Schooled in erotic pleasures, they lived well in the splendor of The Palace.

Each secretly hoped to be The Queen.

Foolishly.

Of course, they were betrayed from the beginning. D'anor would simply dispose of those who no longer pleased him.

In truth, the lives of the damsels were short.

The King fancied variety and *youthful* beauty.

When D'anor grew bored with a girl, she was told she was being honored, and she was to be taken to The King's retreat in the mountains, where she would be among his select few.

Their departure was a splendid show. With lavish ceremony, the two or three chosen would be escorted to a fine coach and carried off toward the manor in the mountains. Eventually, well away from The Capital, they arrived at a bathhouse. Their matron would instruct them to disrobe and remove all their jewelry before bathing in the magic water from the hot springs.

Their jewelry and clothing were gathered and packed in a trunk.

The matron and the trunk returned to The Palace.

The paramours to be wasted were given simple white robes and ordered into a plain, covered wagon. They objected. But it was too late. Under threat of death by sword or dagger, they were forced inside.

The Kingsmen would play jord, and the winner would ride inside with the forsaken. Sometimes, there were scuffles, even fights. But in the end, a winner rode in the wagon. The girls were his. By the threat of death—or the promise of salvation—The Kingsman had his way.

Some of the betrayed would plead.

Some hoped to save themselves by their enthusiastic participation.

No girl was ever spared. The Kingsmen had their orders. Ultimately, the wagon arrived at the point of The Last Dance (as The Kingsmen called it). Here the discarded were dragged screaming to the edge of a cliff and thrown to the rocks a hundred feet below. The Kingsmen watched each girl flailing through the air—The Last Dance. And The Kingsmen laughed.

+++++

In The Council Chamber, D'anor was impatiently listening to the self-aggrandizing speech of The Commander General. The King shifted, leaning forward and then back. He tilted his head back and looked to the ceiling. Then, he looked to the floor and adjusted his mask. D'anor wanted news about the secret society—those who would follow Artama. The King wanted facts.

The Commander General continued orating, "And so, My Lord, my men have been searching . . . and—"

"What do you have to say, Commander?"

"My Lord, Officer Tribb has much to say," the Commander answered, motioning toward the entry to The Chamber.

"Then bring him in and let him say it."

The Commander General turned quickly and walked to the door. He opened it slightly and spoke to one of The Kingsmen on guard. A moment later, the door was opened completely, and Tribb stepped into The Chamber. He advanced several paces and kneeled. "My Lord?"

"Come forward, Officer Tribb."

Tribb rose and walked to the front of The Chamber. He stood erect.

The Commander General returned to his seat between The Jester and The High Priest.

D'anor addressed Tribb. "At some length, The Commander General has told us you have important news about affairs in Eastedge."

"Yes, My Lord."

"Well then, speak."

"My Lord, to begin: There is a secret society—known as The Hope of The Radiant Star. Its purpose is to organize a rebellion."

The members of The Council grumbled to one another. The Commander General leaned toward The High Priest and cursed. The Minister of The Treasury turned to The Minister of Commerce and mumbled, "This will be costly and disruptive to business." The Minister of Education turned to The Minister of Information on his left and angrily demanded, "Why have we not heard of this before?" The Minister of Law muttered, "Treason," his face almost as crimson as his robe. Only The Jester remained silent, keeping his own counsel.

Tribb continued, "This . . . sect . . . is centered in Eastedge, although it is spreading through the realms."

The snarling of The Council grew louder.

The King leaned forward and studied Tribb's face. Although darkened by the sun, Tribb's skin was clear and smooth. D'anor adjusted his mask so it did not rankle the suppurating lesion on his chin and said, "Tell us, Officer Tribb, what is The Radiant Star?"

"*Who*, My Lord?"

"The Radiant Star. What is it?"

"The Radiant Star is . . . ultimately . . . a person, My Lord."

D'anor snapped, "Then, *who* is this person?"

"Artama."

Now, the air was heated with shouted expletives.

D'anor raised his hand, and The Chamber grew quiet. "Artama is the leader of this outrage?"

"No, My Lord," answered Tribb. "I have arrested the leader."

The Council began murmuring again.

Tribb knew this was his moment, and he could not suppress a smile. "I have arrested him and brought him to The Capital. He is now your prisoner."

D'anor was conflicted about this young, clearly ambitious officer, but he rubbed his hands together and said, "Tell me, what is the name of this prisoner?"

"Korbin, My Lord."

The King turned to The Commander General and commanded him, "Have this *Korbin* brought here immediately."

"Absolutely, My Lord." And The Commander General began to move quickly toward the door.

Speculation was rampant among The Council.

The High Priest shouted to The Commander General, "What if this blasphemy of The Hope of The Radiant Star has truly spread throughout the realms? What will you do?"

The Commander turned angrily and replied, "Crush it." Then, he continued walking down the aisle and left The Chamber.

The Minister of Commerce spoke across the aisle to the Minister of The Treasury, "This will bring chaos—commerce will be ruined. What can we do?"

The Minister of The Treasury replied, "Make more d'anors. Give people money. They will spend it."

Conjecturing, The Ministers of Information, Education, and Law huddled together in a cluster of green, dark blue, and crimson. Only The Jester remained silent, keeping his own counsel.

Tribb could see his life changing. "My Lord, may I speak?"

"Continue."

"There is something else." Tribb was in his glory. "I have brought you another person of great value. This man was—dare I say, My Lord—this man was a Reader."

The Council raged in tumult.

"He was a Reader, and he is a friend—" Tribb chuckled sardonically, "he is a friend of Artama—a confidant. He has known Artama since before—again, dare I say, My Lord—since before Artama was The Writer. He knows what Artama is thinking, and he knows his plans."

Again, to quell the turbulence, D'anor raised his hand, and The Council obeyed.

There were three knocks on the door. The door opened slowly. The Commander General stepped inside. He made his way down the aisle and took his seat next to The Jester.

The King sighed. Looking to Tribb, he said, "This friend of Artama—"

"Hape, My Lord."

"What?"

"Hape, My Lord. His name is Hape."

"Where is this *Hape*?"

"In the antechamber, My Lord."

The King turned to The Commander General and ordered, "Have him brought in."

Again, The Commander General rose from his seat, walked up the center aisle, and left The Chamber.

The Jester cleared his throat, and Tribb looked at him. Their eyes met, and they both displayed the slightest smile (both appreciating that The Commander General was running Tribb's errands).

There were three knocks on the door.

D'anor rolled his eyes.

The door opened, and The Commander General entered, followed by the former Reader. "My Lord, this is Hape." Again, The Commander General made his way down the aisle and returned to his seat.

Hape kneeled.

D'anor spoke, "Come forward."

Hape advanced and stood before The King. "My Lord, I am Hape. I was a Reader. And I know Artama well."

"Interesting. And?"

"Information, My Lord."

"You would betray Artama?"

"Out of devotion to My Lord—and my God."

Again, there were three knocks at the door.

The door opened and two Kingsmen, one on each side, led Korbin into The Chamber.

D'anor raised his hand. "Wait." Then he looked to Hape. "Be available at midday tomorrow." He looked to Tribb. "You too, Officer." He waved his hand dismissively and said, "In the meantime, see The Steward. Have him arrange for the satisfaction of your desires—food, drink, women—whatever. Now, leave us."

Thanking and bowing, Hape and Tribb backed away. They turned and walked toward the door. As Hape passed Korbin, he looked away, avoiding Korbin's eyes. As Tribb passed, he glared and smirked.

The Kingsmen led Korbin—in shackles—to the front of The Chamber.

Korbin was filthy. His hair was matted and greasy, fouled with bits of feculent straw. His face was bruised and crusted with dried blood, and his right eye was almost swollen shut. His clothes were as filthy as his hair.

"You stink." D'anor put his hand to the nose of his mask. To The Kingsmen, he ordered, "Move him back until I cannot smell him."

The Kingsmen shuffled Korbin back a few feet.

The King demanded, "What is your name?"

The prisoner was silent.

"You scum!" shouted D'anor.

Everyone flinched, except the captive. He stood impassively.

"You filthy scum!" D'anor began to rant. "You stinking maggot! You have the nerve to defile this Chamber with your rotting presence and not answer when I speak to you?"

The Kingsmen jabbed the prisoner with their cudgels.

"Who are you?" The King demanded again.

Still, the prisoner was silent.

One Kingsman hammered Korbin across his kidneys, and Korbin dropped to his knees, groaning.

"That is a start," scoffed D'anor. "And now, your name?"

"Korbin."

"Korbin—the mighty leader of hope. What is it again? The Hope of The Radiant Star?"

Korbin struggled to stand.

"Stay on your knees, you pig." D'anor took a deep breath. "So, tell me, stinking pig, tell me about your hope."

Korbin remained silent.

The High Priest stood and commanded the prisoner, "You shall answer The King, and you shall address him as *My Lord*."

Korbin spoke—weakly. No one could understand what he said.

"What did you say?" asked The High Priest.

Korbin glared at him, and then, he looked to D'anor. This time, audibly, Korbin said, "He is not *my* Lord."

If there had been uproar before, The Council was now in a furor—a frenzy of outrage in robes of brown, black, green, gray, yellow, blue, and crimson.

The High Priest himself rose from his seat, strode to the prisoner, and spit on him. Standing over Korbin, The High Priest demanded, "Do you acknowledge the one true God to be Nam? Do you acknowledge D'anor, The King, to be the true chosen one of Nam?"

Korbin slowly lifted his head and directed his reply to D'anor. "You are nothing but a despicable tyrant."

The High Priest spit on him again.

The Kingsmen began beating Korbin savagely, mercilessly—one using his cudgel on

Korbin's head and face, the other hitting him repeatedly across his kidneys. A blow to Korbin's mouth broke off three of his teeth.

The Commander General shouted, "Stop!"

The Jester strode to The King and whispered in his ear.

Korbin was sprawled on the floor, blood streaming from his nose and mouth.

The King nodded, and The Jester returned to his seat.

"Remove this heretic, this bleeding pig!" commanded D'anor.

The Kingsmen dragged Korbin toward the doorway by his feet, his face smearing the aisle with blood.

D'anor stood and spoke, "The blasphemy of this pig means his death." D'anor turned to The Commander General. "But he must not know it. You must give him hope. He must think—if he cooperates—he can save himself. He must betray Artama fully. He must betray all his friends. When you are satisfied that he has given all the information we need, deface him and return him to Eastedge for all the people to see. He will be treated like a leper. He will live in disgrace and torment until—in his despair—he will die by his own hand." D'anor coldly scanned the arc of Ministers. "Now, this Council is adjourned."

GRAVITY *forms space and time by mutual attraction.*

One of the four fundamental forces, the phenomenon of objects of mass attracting one another, the consequence of the curvature of space-time, or rather the consequence of mass distorting time-space, creating curvature.

Unlimited range, acting on all particles. It cannot be absorbed or transformed. There is no shield against it.

Although the weakest of the four fundamental forces, gravity is macroscopically dominant, slowly drawing matter together, creating galaxies.

4

IN THE BLUE AND GOLD AND WHITE, Artama heard the resonating chorus, the pure voices, the song everlasting. Exhilarating warmth coursed his spine. Artama was in the moment—in the joy he first knew on E1.

He took another bite of Kora's chocolate.

It seems so long ago, he thought, remembering his last night on that distant world—his last night with Kora. *The pool in the grove of weebon trees—Kora's favorite place. Perpetually filled by a spring, water flowed over rocks, bubbles appeared and merged and burst . . . and the rocks, gradually . . . over vast time . . . had become rounded stones. The trees were covered in silky white cocoons.*

We were seated on the low stone wall surrounding the pool. Kora was playing the meteoron—the strings glimmering in blue and gold and white—and she began to sing:

> *I came for you.*
> *I came for anyone in pain,*
> *And you know I return,*
> *And you know I remain.*
>
> *Do you remember?*
> *A few people do.*
> *As old as the hills . . .*
> *Older than Evil . . .*
> *One Love . . . .*
>
> *I came for you.*
> *I came for anyone in pain,*
> *And you know I return,*
> *And you know I remain.*
>
> *I remember uneven ground . . .*
> *Men looking for gold,*
> *Looking for power,*
> *Looking in vain.*
> *And fallen on the uneven ground*

Were men without gold,
Without power,
Burning,
Crying in vain.

I came for you.
I came for anyone in pain,
And you know I return,
And you know I remain . . .
One Love.

Now, seated at the reading table in the waning light of the fireplace, Artama looked at the meteoron hanging on the wall—the instrument Kora had given him. Although it had been damaged during his return from E1—mostly marring of the finish—the meteoron was beautiful to behold. Similar to a guitar, the instrument had a neck with a fretted fingerboard. The strings were made of meteoron—the most musical of metals—and when played, they glowed in blue and gold and white. The body was made of curlywood, with an intricate swirling grain. Curlywood was not only exquisite in appearance but also gifted a transcendental sound.

That last night, at the pool . . . . The chocolate—the chunk of chocolate. She took a bite and gave me the rest. The cocoons began to quiver, shimmering with golden light.

She removed her necklace, settled it around my neck. The talisman—the gold coin struck with the dragon moon—rested on my chest, gently radiating her warmth. "This will serve you well," she said. "Remember me. Dream of me. Include me in your prayers. I will pray for you." And she added, "Be careful what you reveal."

I walked to the trees to study the cocoons as they split open—the golden incandescence. I focused on one glowing chrysalis. It shook. It lurched. It twitched.

I turned back, but she was gone, her dress laid over the stone wall.

Her head emerged from the water. She laughed and called, "Come in!" and dived below the surface again.

I looked back to the cocoons, then back to the pool.

Kora reappeared. "Come on! We can watch the sunset." She turned away, looking toward the fading golden light. Floating on her back, she tilted her head back into the water and gazed upward—into the purple and gold.

I undressed.

Kora rolled over and dived again.

I stepped onto the wall, facing the pool. The talisman glowed softly. I stood for a moment, took a deep breath, and then dived into the water.

The pool was delightfully comfortable, neither cool nor warm: perfect.

Underwater, our eyes met in deep vision. Everything flowing crystal at the edge. Safe . . . in the moment . . . in the middle of eternity. There was no time. We were . . . there. Floating in the middle of infinity. Immortal.

Lost in Kora's eyes, I saw E3 orbiting my sun, saw the dragon moon orbiting E3. I saw clearly . . . eternally . . . infinitely . . . now.

On that last night, another split cocoon trembled, and ever so slowly, a glorious golden butterfly emerged. One by one, the cocoons opened, and as night fell, the weebon trees glowed in the aura of the metamorphoses. The golden butterflies lifted, swimming apparently erratically into the night.

Now, the glowing embers gave the only light, and a chill shuddered Artama.

Flash of red . . . splash of blood.

More often, the visions come unexpectedly now.

Korbin in a cell, doubled over, gasping for breath. Face crusted with scabs. Fresh blood running from his nose. Wearing no shirt, body bruised and welted. Hands shackled behind his back. A Kingsman hits him again with a cudgel, and Korbin drops to the floor, all brightness gone from his eyes—only resoluteness remains.

Melancholy washed over Artama.

In a sense, I know I am responsible for Korbin's torment. All this anguish flows from my decision—as a boy—to cross The Plain.

When Artama returned the first time—with the ointment Kora had given him—he was able to cure his father's blindness, and he was honored by everyone. He was proclaimed The Writer, tasked with writing in *The Book of Knowledge & Wisdom.*

Wanting only to bring hope and enlightenment, he wrote the truth and noble thoughts.

But most people were interested in something else.

As the tale was repeatedly told, it was embellished with every telling until the people believed Artama knew the path to gold beyond imagination.

In time, this brought Zortan and his beastly horde.

To save The Town, Artama led Zortan away—onto The Plain.

He knew he could not lead him *across. Crossing* is a matter of the heart.

Artama knew his survival was unlikely.

But he was saved . . . by the dragons.

And through the watchtower portal, he crossed the second time to E1, the realm of knowledge and wisdom . . . and Kora.

I know my decision to cross The Plain was the result of an endless flow of inscrutable precedent events—each as much the cause of Korbin's fate as my decision.

Yet Artama felt the sadness. The Town was saved, but the fear of new marauders infected the people, and they gladly accepted the promises of D'anor.

Many now despised Artama, holding him responsible for their circumstances, holding him responsible for their lives. Others revered him as a holy man. Others, like Korbin, wanted Artama to lead a rebellion.

Returning to E3 the second time was more difficult than expected, although he had been warned. On E1, The Academy Master of Swordsmanship, Antag, had counseled: "We practice the sword as a discipline, for the sake of discipline. Focus. Concentration. To keep strong and alert. But *you—Artama*—will need these skills in fights for your life."

There had already been the encounter with the bandits on The Plain.

On E1, Artama had studied diligently, and he had the vocabulary to discuss the countless notions regarding the origin of life and the path to ultimate fulfillment. Some of the notions were religions—polytheistic, pantheistic, monotheistic—and most were held to be the only true notion by their adherents. Artama had studied Aboriginal Dreaming, The Eternal Prophet, Braxism, Confucianism, Taoism, Buddhism, Shenism, Judaism, Christianity, Sunni Islam, Shi'a Islam, Sufism, Hinduism, Jainism, Animism, Shinto, The Elegant, and Voodoo . . . . The list seemed endless.

Artama was at peace with a belief in One Love—The One.

Clearly, the religion of D'anor—Namism—was merely an insubstantial fiction, a tool of manipulation and coercion.

And Artama knew the sword was not the answer—though often required.

If given a choice, Artama would choose a contemplative life, but he knew that was not to be. After all, Thorne himself had given him The Crystal.

I cannot lead a successful rebellion against the power of D'anor—but I may cause a revolution . . . of thinking, of understanding.

Artama believed in the ultimate reunion of each soul with The One.

But why the separation?

Seated at the reading table, Artama poured water from a pitcher into a cup and noted the bubbles: For a moment, they appeared, tended to gather and merge, and at last, they burst—becoming one with the air.

Although the bubbles are separated from each other and the air in the room, eventually every bubble will burst . . . human separation will disappear, and each will be One. To be human is to be separated—samsara. To be One is to no longer be human—moksha.

Another wave of melancholy . . . as Artama saw farther into the future, witnessing the beginning of Korbin's defacement. Life on E3 had fogged his ability to vision clearly—and he was not able to direct his visions with the precision he had mastered on E1—but he could still glimpse.

More often, the visions come unexpectedly now.

A Kingsman heating an iron rod unto glowing red. The rod is the circumference of a man's finger and about two feet in length. Korbin is bound to a table, his head strapped so it cannot move. With a heavily gloved hand, the Kingsman removes the glowing rod from the fire and pushes it into Korbin's face. Korbin screams, and the Kingsman removes the rod.

Then, he does it again.

The process would take some time: a few deep burns each day until the victim's face was gone, nothing left but a mass of horrifying holes and scar tissue—unrecognizable as human. Eventually, the defaced wretch would be released into the population to wander as an example to everyone. Helping the defaced was a risk—The Kingsmen took note and kept a record, and those who helped were watched more closely. Consequently, the defaced, commonly, did not live long—victims of their weakened condition and subsequent neglect. In their isolation, many committed suicide.

In miraculous eternity, why such brutality?

Does The One hold compassion for each individual—each separated soul?

The perception of separation manifests in doubt.

After all of Artama's conversations with The Headmaster and Kora—after all of his conscientious studies and meditations—the question remained: Why the suffering of innocents?

But who is innocent?

Who is guilty?

No one knows his next thought. What will it be? From where? Why?

Artama did not understand the blindness of humankind to the wonder, the miracle of creation. He could not understand the avarice, the hatred, the lust for power.

A chill swept over him. He envisioned his writings—the sheets of lapa—scattered across the dust and blowing away in the wind. There was an indistinguishable figure riding away madly on a horse.

Other than himself, only four people knew of the writings: the three former Readers and his father. But he had a sickening feeling the writings were in danger. He thought about going to The Hall, but he knew it was foolishly unsafe. He would undoubtedly attract attention. There were always Kingsmen on patrol.

By the grace of D'anor.

To live quietly, peacefully . . . or to die violently, valiantly in battle for a righteous cause—what does one man do?

Revenant, liminal, retrocognate Artama knew he was merely stardust—yet glorious stardust.

What does one man do? Resist, if only for honor?

Artama knew he had no prophecy to fulfill, and in that sense, he was free.

He rose from his seat at the reading table and checked that the drapes were drawn completely closed. He walked to the large cabinet—where the glazing supplies were kept—on the far wall, next to the archway separating the private workshop from the production shop. He quietly moved the cabinet out from the wall—just enough that he could get behind it—and carefully removed three boards from the back. Inside was a leather satchel and a scabbard. He removed the scabbard and slowly withdrew the invisible blade. He felt the weight and balance. He raised it, swinging left and right, distorting the air. On E3, Artama and his father were the only two people who knew.

Except the two bandits who attacked me on The Plain. But they had no idea . . . and who would believe them?

Artama sheathed The Crystal and returned the scabbard to its hiding place. He replaced the boards and pushed the cabinet back against the wall.

Back at the reading table, Artama rewrapped what remained of Kora's chocolate and returned it to the wooden box where he kept the things he cherished: the nutshell containing the amber ointment, the map, the needlebox, the telescope, the lighter, the jar of golden ointment, the candle, and the gold coin.

No matter the choice I make, people will die.

He removed the candle, remembering Kora's words: *"Because a candle flame is a constant in our worlds."* He rarely lit it. When it was gone, it would be gone forever. But he lit it now.

His forehead was suddenly radiant.

Her kiss.

He inhaled the fragrance redolent of miraculous healing. He could feel her breathing.

It was quiet. Nothing was ever more quiet: the quiet of the moment before The Beginning, before The Singularity.

Artama walked to the meteoron hanging on the wall. He took it down, went back to his seat, and began to play. In Kora's candlelight, the vibrating strings glimmered in blue and gold and white. The music was magic.

Artama began to sing:

> I miss you.
> In the morning, you were cheerful
>   and bright.
> I miss you.
> In the darkness, you were my
>   candlelight.
> Plain and simple—black and white:
> This empty space is your place.
> I miss you.

THE UNIVERSE *is without size, ineffably, mostly invisible—dark matter and dark energy.*

Although dark matter is unseen, the gravitational effects are apparent. There is not enough visible mass to hold galaxies together.

Dark energy comprises the vast majority of the universe, invisibly permeating it, accelerating its expansion until gravity and other forces are overcome, material objects are rent asunder, and matter is so thinly dispersed that there is nothing again.

Until the emergence of a new universe.

5

TO THE NORTHWEST OF THE CAPITAL, across the river, on the eastern slope of The Dragon Mountain, grew The Forest of Fire (so named for the red leaves of the dragon trees—trees unknown elsewhere in The Kingdom).

Here began the making of d'anors.

+++++

In the morning, The King was at The Treasury, observing the making of money, consulting with The Minister of The Treasury and The Minister of Commerce—and The Jester. The Minister of The Treasury was speaking, but the thoughts of D'anor were thoughts of Artama— damnable Artama. The King was preoccupied with the memory of The Minister of Information in The Council: "There is increasing talk of a growing secret society of those who would follow him against you. More and more are claiming he is holy—resurrected." Distractedly, D'anor asked The Minister of The Treasury, "Should we raise taxes?"

But it was The Minister of Commerce who spoke first. "My Lord, I fear raising taxes would cause further discontent."

The King remembered the words of Tribb: "There is a secret society—known as The Hope of The Radiant Star. Its purpose is to organize rebellion."

The Jester spoke, "My Lord, of course, we have no need to tax. We can make all the money we want."

The King was thinking about the prisoner—Korbin.

The Jester continued, "We only tax to help them believe. We *should* raise taxes—if only to maintain the illusion of value."

"And pass new money among them to ease the burden," added The Minister of The Treasury.

"It makes no sense," said D'anor.

"But it works, My Lord," replied The Jester.

"So be it, then," commanded The King.

+++++

Guarding The Forest of Fire was the occupation of many Kingsmen. Sentries were stationed around the perimeter, and more Kingsmen, on horses, patrolled the interior. Entry and departure were absolutely regulated. No unauthorized travel was permitted. Under penalty of defacement.

A dragon tree typically grew to the height of ten men. Reaching around the trunk, a man could not quite touch his hands, and the limbs also began just beyond his reach. In the afternoon sunlight, viewed from below, the fiery leaves created a rutilant crown canopy.

Working in the oppressively humid heat after the recent rain, slaves labored under the cold, suspicious eyes of Kingsmen. The Forest Manager selected the trees to be taken. The slaves sawed endlessly—first felling the trees and then cutting the trunks and limbs into manageable sections.

Next, the bark was harvested—stripped from the wood in sheets. The sheets were stacked flat on elaborately decorated carts. The wood was loaded onto larger, plain wagons. Both the bark and the wood were destined for delivery to The Capital—the bark to The Treasury, the wood to feed the fires of The Palace and the forge.

At the river, the decorated carts and plain wagons were driven onto separate barges and secured. Four Kingsmen on horseback rode theatrically onto each barge carrying bark. The barges carrying wood were unguarded. Each ferry was connected by ropes to both sides of the river and was pulled back and forth across the current by slaves.

Whenever the elaborately decorated carts loaded with bark rumbled through the gate in the outer wall of The Capital, adults and children alike stopped to watch. The

Kingsmen sat arrogantly erect, and their mounts seemed to prance insolently.

In The Treasury, craftsmen laid sheets of bark on large tables and began separating the bark from a membrane of soft material on the inside. Very carefully, the bark was peeled away, leaving a sheet of translucent *green gold*, the material that became d'anors.

While the sheets of green gold were still moist, they were hung over racks and taken to the imprinting room. Here, again laid on tables, they were carefully inspected. Flawed areas were removed with blades and taken away to be fed to the fire.

Workers measured and—with blue ink—laid out a grid of lines on each sheet, creating rectangles a little smaller than a man's hand. Other workers—with cork-tipped tools—printed dots of blood-red dye at each corner of each rectangle. The dye would soak into the translucent green gold and spread into a circular spot.

Next—amid the intoxicating fragrances of green gold, red dye, and blue ink—a senior craftsman would imprint the image of D'anor—the court mask of D'anor—into the center of each rectangle. Then, in blue ink, beneath the mask, another senior craftsman stamped the words *By The Grace of D'anor.*

Eventually, an officer of The Treasury, using the blue ink, imprinted a number into the red spots on the upper left and upper right corners of each rectangle—the value. Today, the number was 10. Not long ago, it was 5.

Next, another officer of The Treasury imprinted The King's seal into the red spot on the lower right corner. And finally, another officer, after carefully inspecting each rectangle, would impress his seal into the red spot on the lower left corner.

The sheets were again hung over racks and taken to a warehouse to dry.

Then, they were cut along the grid lines and became bills, currency: inexhaustible money—as long as the dragon trees grew in

The Forest of Fire—as long as there were larger numbers to stamp on each bill—as long as there were Kingsmen to enforce the will of D'anor.

+++++

At midday, standing before The King in The Royal Chamber, standing beside Tribb, Hape was tempted to reveal his knowledge of Artama's writings. On the other hand, he knew—to reap the greatest benefit—he should wait. He should be patient. He knew Artama was writing about warfare, and Artama had once explained *explosives* as weapons. Even what Artama called *primitive* explosives could bring the overwhelming defeat of D'anor and all his Kingsmen. But if The King had the knowledge, he would be invincible—and Hape would be invaluable.

Standing before The King, standing beside Hape, Tribb was worried: Had his value fallen—now that D'anor knew Hape? Now that Korbin was in the dungeon? Tribb needed trouble. He needed at least the appearance of a rebellion. He needed a reason for a victory—a reason to defeat Artama, a reason to kill him.

+++++

The fat clown with the painted smiling face (the wizard with the nutshells and the pea) was delighted to be back in The Capital. The clientele was better and the available diversions far superior: The gamblers had more money to lose; the food and drink were excellent; and the women were more appealing.

+++++

Outside the workshop, in the warmth of the afternoon sun, Artama was talking with a group of travelers gathered around him. Most came to buy pottery. Some were interested in learning about life beyond The Plain—life on E1. Many wanted to discuss the arrest of Korbin.

All such gatherings were potentially dangerous: Any traveler—any apparent pilgrim—could be an agent of The King. Artama had to speak guardedly.

Throughout the realms, communication was by spoken word and, therefore, unreliable, subject to inaccurate memory, confused recounting, and strange interpretations. Artama answered the same questions time and time again, always attempting to answer the unanswerable. Artama knew his mission.

"Is life on E1 life after death?" inquired an old man.

"No, E1 is a place in time. People live and die there. In general, they are at peace with the transition."

"I am concerned about the here and now," called a young man. "Now that Korbin has been arrested, what do we do?"

"We must fight," another young man shouted.

We could make explosives, black powder—saltpeter, sulfur, and charcoal. It would take time to gather the ingredients and organize the warriors. Risks would be great—many would die—and in the end, nothing would change.

Artama had studied revolutions and the rise and fall of nations.

To the combative young man, Artama replied, "Although sometimes necessary, fighting is not the answer."

"What *is* the answer?" a woman asked.

Artama remembered being on The Plain, returning from E1, and he remembered Kora singing in his dream:

>*You fell—*
>
>*And felt forsaken—*
>
>*On the white stone,*
>
>*Where the wind blew everywhere.*
>
>*Dust filled the air.*
>
>*The light began to fade,*
>
>*But you are not alone.*

Artama replied, "An innocence of heart . . . of spirit. Love—without dogma—One Love."

+++++

In The Royal Chamber, The Jester walked to The King and whispered in his ear. D'anor nodded, and The Jester walked away.

The King addressed Tribb, "It would have been better, Officer, if you had continued monitoring these clandestine meetings—gathering information. In a sense, we have been blinded."

Then, D'anor turned to Hape and said, "I want *you* to maintain a relationship with Artama. Feed me information."

Turning back to Tribb, The King declared, "That will be all."

Now—more than ever—Hape was resolved not to reveal Artama's writings—until the time was right.

Tribb's worst fear was becoming a reality: He had squandered potential of incalculable value by giving away Korbin and Hape.

Tribb bowed and was about to take his leave, but he stopped. "My Lord, may I briefly speak?"

"What is it?"

"My Lord, thank you for your many blessings." Tribb paused. "May I recommend a treat for you from Eastedge?"

"And what would this treat be?" asked D'anor, always suspicious but always hungry.

"A lovely morsel of a girl."

D'anor chuckled.

"She lives in the south quarter, in the cottage of her father, Jaspon. He is well-known as a maker of tools. She is well-known for her beauty . . . and she is just becoming a woman. She would not be hard to locate."

"And her name, Officer?"

"Cressa."

"I am always looking to add beauty to The Palace."

"Good day, My Lord." Tribb bowed, stood erect, turned, and made his way out of The Royal Chamber, hoping he had salvaged his relationship with The King.

+++++

That night, Artama beheld the firmament—starlight in his eyes, stardust in his bones—

contemplating *Bodhisattva*: the awakening warrior—one who has attained full Enlightenment—one who has attained *prajna* but postpones *Nirvana* (out of love and compassion) to help others attain it.

Another chill swept over him, and he again envisioned his writings scattered across the dust, blowing away in the wind, the indistinguishable figure riding away madly . . . .

Artama remembered the conclusion of the song Kora sang in his dream on The Plain:

> *You fell—*
> *And felt forsaken—*
> *On the black stone,*
> *Where the wind blew everywhere.*
> *Overcome by despair,*
> *As though morning were delayed,*
> *But you are not alone.*
>
> *A perfect half, I held you,*
> *Until you could laugh,*
> *Where the wind blew everywhere.*

You are not alone.

We are not alone.

At that moment, Artama shuddered in frisson—knowing Kora would soon be with him.

+++++

In candlelight, wearing his golden mask, D'anor sat at his dressing table, staring at the mirror. It had been a tiresome day, and he was in a foul mood. The morning at The Treasury had been tedious, and the time spent in the afternoon with Hape and Tribb had been unsatisfyingly inconclusive—Artama remained a problem. Framing the mirror, hanging on hooks, were seventeen other masks—five above the mirror and five below, with four on the left side and three on the right. On the right, there was one empty hook. The masks served different occasions—from formal to ribald. D'anor removed tonight's mask—a somber, intimidating visage—and hung it on the empty hook. The candlelight reflecting from the gold of the masks was splendid, but the image in the mirror was abhorrent. D'anor beheld his face—horrendously scarred from a lifetime of oozing pustules. His youth had been a daily torment of self-loathing. Over the years, many healers from many lands had tried, but nothing could be done—none were successful. D'anor was cursed.

But he was The King.

+++++

In his bedchamber, The Jester sat at his dressing table, removing his makeup. Looking in the mirror, he watched his face gradually appear as he wiped away his black-on-white face paint. His mask changed strategically from day to day—sometimes from hour to hour—from comic to sober to intimidating to tragic, limited only by his boundless creativity.

The Jester was no fool: He was handsome beneath his masks, and—master that he was—he artfully distracted D'anor from noticing. No good ever came from arousing The King's jealousy.

When his face was clean, The Jester smiled at himself in the mirror. He chuckled and said: "We are *truly* alchemists—turning tree bark into gold."

OVER TIME, *gravity causes the atoms of gases and space dust to coalesce, and by accretion from the solar nebula, a circumstellar disk appears.*

Gases and dust gather into asteroids and planetesimals and planetoids, colliding and colliding, becoming larger, eventually becoming planets.

Radioactive heat and the aftershocks of collisions create a molten mass.

In time, the mass cools and becomes rock—on the surface.

On this surface—upon this rock— creatures may one day roam.

6

KORA WAS FLOATING naked in the pool in the grove of weebon trees, admiring the firmament—starlight in her eyes, stardust in her bones.

Silently, transports and shuttles passed overhead—lights challenging the stars. The two moons of E1 were bright in the night.

The pool was perpetually filled by the spring. Water flowed over rocks, bubbles appeared and merged and burst, and the rocks, gradually, over vast time, had become rounded stones. The water was clear and comfortable.

Kora—a strong swimmer, slender yet powerful—resumed swimming, backstroking gracefully. Swimming eased the yearning, the melancholy. Kora rolled into the breaststroke and swam to the edge of the pool. She climbed the stone steps, took her towel, and wrapped herself in it—her wet, black hair darker than the night. She sat on the low stone wall and gazed at the weebon trees. Kora thought about her last night with Artama. How long had it been? Not a day passed that she did not think of him. Tonight, the weebon trees were unadorned, unlike that night when they were covered in silky white cocoons.

On that night, Kora remembered saying, "We always knew this time would come. We always knew you would return."

"You know I want to stay," said Artama.

"And I know you must return."

They embraced.

In time, Kora stepped back, took Artama by the hand, and guided him to the pack and the meteoron case. They sat on the wall.

Kora said, "The Headmaster has attended to your survival. You will have water and food and a blanket and a lighter. And a map, of course. And The Crystal." Kora brightened. "I have packed a few other things for you as well."

She opened the pack and removed a neatly folded scarf. Unfolding it revealed a block of chocolate. She broke off a chunk, took a small bite, and gave the rest to Artama. Transcending bittersweetness.

Kora removed a nutshell containing the amber ointment, the salve Artama had used to heal his father's blindness. "The nutshell is a token of the first time."

Then, she removed a small jar. She opened it, and the jar emitted a golden glow. "The golden ointment, of course."

Artama put his hand to his forehead, touching the radiant scar that was to become the symbol of his destiny.

Next, Kora removed a candle. "Because a candle flame is a constant in our worlds."

And finally, she removed the needlebox. "Still useful."

Artama smiled, remembering the simple words chanted in The Readings in The Hall in The Town:

> *When you are lost—and cannot*
> *decide—*
> *Let the needlebox be your guide.*
> *The needlebox always points the*
> *way home.*

Kora began repacking. "There are a couple of surprises at the bottom." She smiled. "Some of these things you will need, others you will simply be glad you have, one will be lost along the way." She winked and closed the pack.

On that final night, Artama removed the meteoron from its case and began playing, the strings glimmering in blue and gold and white.

Tears came to Kora's eyes.

Cocoons were beginning to shudder—one began to split, radiating a gentle golden glow.

The gold of the sun was deepening, and the purple clouds stretched across the sky.

Artama sang:

>I remember,
>
>Before I came,
>
>Before my name and number.
>
>I remember, and I dream.

>Like a memory,
>
>I wander around
>
>Looking for you—
>
>Finding my way home.
>
>Beyond the blue and gold and
>>white,
>
>From the moment before
>
>The perfect crystal sunlight
>
>Began shining—
>
>Seemingly, for evermore . . . .

>Like a memory,
>
>I wander around
>
>Looking for you—
>
>Finding my way home.

>I remember,

Before I came,

Before my name and number.

I remember, and I dream.

More cocoons opened incandescently. The purple clouds grew darker.

Artama leaned the meteoron against the wall.

Kneeling before him, Kora lifted the gold chain over her head and settled it around Artama's neck. The talisman—the gold coin struck with the dragon of the dragon moon—now rested on Artama's chest. It held Kora's warmth. "This will serve you well," she said. "Remember me. Dream of me. Include me in your prayers. I will pray for you."

"I will."

"Be careful what you reveal."

Another split cocoon trembled, and-- ever so slowly—a glorious butterfly emerged.

Kora and Artama dived below the surface, and their eyes met in deep vision. Everything was flowing crystal at the edge. They were safe . . . in the moment . . . in the middle of eternity. There was no time. They were . . . *there.* Floating in the middle of infinity. Immortal.

One by one, the cocoons opened, and as night fell, the weebon trees glowed in the aura of the metamorphoses. The golden butterflies lifted, fluttering apparently erratically into the night.

Now, sitting alone wrapped in a towel, Kora shuddered with the chill of a vision: Artama's writings were scattered across the dust and blowing away in the wind. There was an indistinguishable figure riding away . . . .

Kora knew it was time to talk with her father.

+++++

In The Great Hall of The Academy of Anagnorisis, in the large antechamber of The Headmaster's office, Kora was seated in a high-backed upholstered chair, waiting in unsettled anticipation. Her hands were in her lap. Then, she moved them to the arms of the chair.

Then, she moved them back to her lap and intertwined her fingers.

On a window ledge, a cat was sleeping in the golden afternoon sunlight.

Kora considered the room. She had been here many, many times. The golden glowing windows (where the cat slept) were to the left. The windows were tall, and the entire wall was aglow. The cat was the color of the dust of The Plain, and its whiskers were golden. Immediately before Kora was the door to The Headmaster's office—a heavy, dark wooden door carved with dragons and swirling fire. To the right were bookcases—tall, dark wooden bookcases filled with ancient volumes. In front of one of the bookcases was a circular table, and on the table were three globes—E1, E2, and E3—each with a different pattern of blue and green and tan and white, each nested in a dark wooden stand carved with the fire of dragons.

Kora stood and walked toward the table.

The cat awoke and stretched lazily. Then, noticing Kora, it jumped down from the window ledge.

Kora looked at the globe of E3, focusing on a particular area of tan.

The cat rubbed against her ankles.

"Elladora, my sweetheart." Kora stooped, picked up the cat, and cuddled it.

Elladora began to purr.

The door opened, and a tall man in an official black robe smiled and said, "Miss Kora, The Headmaster can see you now." He held out his arms.

Kora put the cat on the floor. "Bradle, it is always good to see you." Stepping forward, she hugged him.

"Likewise, Miss Kora, it is always my pleasure."

The cat scooted through the open doorway into The Headmaster's office.

Kora followed.

Bradle closed the door, remaining in the antechamber. He walked to the windows and stood in the warmth of the sun, looking across the campus of The Academy. After a moment, he turned and walked to the table of globes. Bradle had long served Headmaster Thorne, and he had known Kora from her infancy. He had also known Artama—and became fond of him—while the young man studied at The Academy. Bradle lifted the globe of E3 from its stand, and, as he turned it, his eyes were drawn to the special area of tan. He tossed the globe—spinning it—above his head and caught it. Then he returned it to the stand. He crossed the room again to the windows. Closing his eyes—seeing only orange—he absorbed the warmth of the sun. He inhaled deeply and then exhaled in a long sigh.

He knew.

In The Headmaster's chamber, wearing a robe of the deepest blue, Thorne was seated behind his large wooden desk. His smile was kindly. His hair and beard were white and long. The lines around his eyes were as deep, artful grooves in a pattern on pottery. He rose from his chair, stepped forward, and embraced Kora.

"Father."

"My dear, you are cold." His daughter shivered in his arms. He held her, warming her.

"Father, I seek your blessing."

Thorne stepped back and motioned for Kora to take a seat in one of the high-backed upholstered chairs in front of his desk. He returned to his seat.

He knew this day would come.

Thorne poured water from a pitcher into a cup. He leaned forward and passed the cup to Kora. He poured water into a second cup for himself, noting the bubbles: For a moment, they appeared, tended to gather and merge, and at last, they burst—becoming one with the air.

Kora, holding her cup in both hands, sipped.

Thorne turned his cup back and forth, watching the bubbles disappear. At last, he took a sip.

Kora said, "I want to go to Artama."

Thorne set his cup on his desk, leaned back, and sighed. He leaned forward, his elbows on his desk, and pressed his fingertips to his temples. After some time, he said, "I would dismiss this notion immediately . . . if it were not Artama."

Elladora jumped onto Kora's lap and settled. "Artama and I have known each other since we were little more than children."

Thorne nodded.

"On our first encounter, I was taken with his curiosity, his intelligence—his bravery."

Thorne stroked his beard.

"I gave him the nutshell filled with the amber ointment to heal his father's eyes upon his return to his world."

"And back on E3, he was viewed with awe," said Thorne.

Kora continued, "Later, when he returned to E1, I was stunned by his ignorance—his lack of knowledge regarding basic facts and concepts. Even the notion of gravity was unknown to him. But he was passionately curious."

"And wise," Thorne added. "Although young, an old soul."

"He was blazing with a desire to learn."

"He was selected because *you* praised him," The Headmaster reminded his daughter.

"He absorbed everything." Kora stroked Elladora's jaw.

"And became a legend at The Academy."

"Father, we are soul mates."

"Kora, I remind you: E3 is primitive beyond imagination. The people live like animals—even worse. People are defaced and beheaded."

Elladora jumped down from Kora's lap.

"He is always on my mind."

The cat jumped onto Thorne's lap, and he caressed her.

"I love him, Father."

"I know."

"I want to be with him. I want to *save* him."

Thorne was silent.

Kora continued, "As you have said, 'He has no prophecy to fulfill.'"

Thorne's silence continued. He stroked Elladora. Finally, he said, "Bring him back—he is not required to be a sacrifice."

Kora jumped to her feet and dashed around Thorne's desk. She was radiant.

Elladora jumped down, and Thorne stood.

Father and daughter hugged.

Thorne leaned back and said, "You must begin training for the rigors of E3. This will be exhausting." He shook his head. "We will monitor the situation. At the highest level, we can help—if we have time—if we see a coming catastrophe . . . which I fully expect." Thorne sighed. "At the lowest level, the perils are myriad. Something as simple as the bite of a poisonous spider or a fall from a horse . . . . You will need to become skilled in riding. Any kind of accident—and you could die before we could help. To say nothing of The Kingsmen."

"I know."

Thorne stepped back. "I will be in contact with Antag at the Oron Center. He will see to it that you are instructed in survival skills. Kora, you are a strong young woman, but just as Artama was ignorant of so much when he was a boy, you are without knowledge or skill in matters of primitive survival. There is much to be done."

Tears welled up in Kora's eyes. "Thank you, Father."

GOLD.

In a flash of light so bright the galaxy is overwhelmed, neutron stars collide.

Most of the material collapses to form a black hole. Some is spewed into space, rich in neutrons, driving the formation of the heavy elements.

Gold, dust in the wind, is included in a cloud—materials eventually coalescing into a solar system.

The heavy metals move to the core of the molten planet, and the core becomes heavy with gold.

Later, impacting meteors deliver more to the surface—the surface upon which creatures may one day roam.

7

IN THE DARKNESS, Tribb rode alone in the violent storm. Lightning struck explosively—so close the thunderous crack was immediate—illuminating the landscape with brilliance greater than the sun. In that instant, Tribb saw The Honeycomb—a vast region of countless caves.

Tribb rode into the wind, soaked and shivering, the hood of his capote providing little protection from the rain pelting his face. His usual thoughts of vanquishing Artama were displaced by thoughts of a warm fire, a dry blanket, and mulled weebon wine warming his throat.

Tribb knew he was not far from the infamous inn—The Berry—on the outskirts of Crossroads. There he would spend the night, continuing to Eastedge in the morning. In the meantime, he could only curse the wind and rain.

+++++

Inside The Berry, in the golden light of the fireplaces, the crowd was in high spirits, drinking and laughing, enjoying the camaraderie of being together in comfort, sheltered from the storm.

When a traveler entered the inn through the front door, he would find a huge room. On the walls to the left and right were large, stone fireplaces—and tonight, the fires were blazing. The traveler could walk down a center aisle straight to the bar where tempting barmaids were ready to please. On either side of the aisle were rows of long tables with benches. Tonight, the benches were filled with hungry, thirsty customers. The tabletops were covered with plates of food and flagons of weebon wine. The aromas of roasted pork, chicken, onions, and freshly baked bread combined into a savory delight. Serving wenches flirted and strutted through the crowd.

+++++

In the storm, Tribb rode in miserable desolation.

+++++

Canter was the owner of The Berry, and he and his wife (and his daughter) enjoyed a thriving business. Tonight was an especially good night. Those who may have otherwise pressed on to their ultimate destinations were especially thankful for shelter, and local patrons, who had come to hear the bards and drink, had an excuse for lingering—the deluge.

Canter welcomed bards, minstrels, troubadours, jugglers, magicians—anyone who could attract a crowd. As long as an entertainer could please the patrons, he could have a room, a bath, and a daily meal—all for free—for as long as a week. Wine was provided by the generosity of the paying customers, and the entertainers usually drank well.

The Berry was well-known among the itinerant showmen, and, as they worked their circuit, frequently, more than one would arrive at the same time. Canter's policy was simple: One could stay for free—only one. The paying patrons would decide.

+++++

Through the chilling darkness, Tribb saw the warm light from The Berry, and he spurred his horse with a vengeance.

+++++

On this night, there were two bards at the inn. One, the younger of the two, with blond hair and blue eyes (highly unusual), was singing and playing a lute. He was standing in front of the bar in the open area at the end of the aisle.

There were few women among the crowd, except those working. The serving wenches and barmaids were paid by Canter. The others were on their own. But like the other entertainers, Canter knew they were good for business.

The front door swung open and banged against the wall. Lightning flashed, thunder exploded, and rain blew into the room. Tribb stood in the doorway, glaring.

The young bard stopped playing, and the crowd turned toward the entrance.

Canter made his way quickly across the room to Tribb. "Welcome, sir." Canter closed the door. He called out to his daughter, "Bring a blanket!" The girl hurried off down a hallway. Canter yelled to a serving wench, "Mulled wine! Bring a flagon for The Kingsman!" To his wife, now at his side, he said, "Have the stable boy tend to the officer's horse."

Tribb threw back his hood.

"Come, sit by the fire," said Canter, and he led the way to the fireplace on the right side of the room. As he approached the fire, two men rose from their bench and shuffled away. Tribb removed his capote and sat, tossing the soaked garment onto the bench beside him. Canter's daughter arrived with the blanket. Tribb took it and wrapped himself. The serving wench arrived with a flagon of mulled wine and a cup. She filled the cup and handed it to Tribb. He drained it immediately. She gave him the flagon.

The bard began to play, continuing his song, and the people began to talk again.

Tribb and Canter engaged in a brief conversation, Canter nodding his head, clearly understanding and agreeing.

When the bard finished his song, Canter walked to the front of the room and addressed the assemblage: "As is our usual practice when we are honored with two entertainers, we will have a competition."

Cheers rose from the crowd.

"As is our custom, the winner will get a free room—and a hot meal. The loser, normally, can get anything he can pay for."

The people laughed.

"But tonight, Officer Tribb is in need of a room, and, although the inn is filled, he shall have one, meaning the losing bard will forgo his room and sleep in the stable."

Many in the crowd chuckled. Many felt a chill.

Tribb was watching Canter's daughter as she made her way back and forth. She was young, not yet hardened by her life, and, although rather plain, she reminded Tribb of Cressa—a girl becoming a woman.

Canter concluded with a sweep of his arm toward the young bard with the uncommon blue eyes. "Let the competition begin."

The crowd applauded.

The young bard, eagerly accepting the challenge, intoned:

> Well, then, my newfound friends, I
> shall begin
> This battle of verse I intend to win.
> Outside, the rain is a chilling, dark
> plight,
> But I plan to be warm in a room
> tonight.

One of the young working women called out, "I'll keep you warm."

The audience laughed.

The bard winked at the woman and continued:

> Drink more wine and incline an ear

toward me.
Raise your cups to the famous
history
Of Artama—who crossed The Plain
and returned—
A sojourn never before sojourned.
Men and women raised their cups and
drank.

Tonight, I will remind you in my
rhyme
Of young Artama's return the first
time,
When he brought the miraculous
ointment
And cured his father's crippling
ailment—
Healing Alagon's longtime sightless
eyes.
And like a resplendent springtime
sunrise,
The old blind man could once again
see,
And young Artama sealed his

destiny.

"Praise him!" shouted a woman in the crowd.

Tribb tightened the blanket around his shoulders. Then, he emptied another cup of wine. He filled it again from the flagon.

The blue-eyed bard continued:

> Artama spoke of a golden fountain,
> The water shining silver in the sun.
> He spoke of Kora, the wonderful girl
> Across The Plain on another world.
> Artama spoke of matters of the
> > heart,
> But for all the wisdom he ached to
> > impart—
> No matter what the people were
> > told—
> Most only imagined coffers of gold.

"I could use a handful of coins myself," a man shouted, and there were cheers from many.

> In time, Artama's bold tales brought
> > Zortan,

And, so, Artama's second journey
    began.
Zortan commanded an unholy
    horde,
Men who lived and died by fire—
    and by sword—
Who cared only for glittering gold,
Reptilian men who were deadly
    cold,
Yet worshipped the flames of a
    raging fire.
Gleaming gold—or blood—was their
    only desire.

The audience began to quiet. Older people remembered, and younger people had heard the tale.

To save The Town, Artama led
    Zortan away,
And Alagon watched in anxious
    dismay
As his son vanished over the
    horizon,
Followed by Zortan and the dragon-

men.
Now, the people were almost silent.

In time—the second time—Artama
returned
And told new tales of what he had
learned.
He spoke of fiery dragons saving
him
From his doubt, when it was
hopelessly grim.
He spoke of many strange, amazing
things:
Pure voices singing—as only spirits
sing—
And how the harmony reverberated.
He spoke of the wisdom celebrated
At The Academy where he studied,
Where his body and mind and soul
were freed.
He spoke of the one he came to
adore—a
Young woman now—his wonderful
Kora.

"Now you're talking!" a man shouted.

The working women leaned into any man they were near.

> People want to know how to cross
>> The Plain,
> And Artama patiently tries to
>> explain:
> From the beginning, from the very
>> start,
> The journey is a matter of the heart.
> But the tale is age-old and oft
>> retold:
> Most people just care about finding
>> gold—
> Although some would seek The
>> Academy,
> And others long for immortality.
> Personally, I would be looking for a
> Lover of my own, my own sweet
>> Kora.

The crowd loved it, and they cheered and banged their cups on the tables.

The young balladeer said, "Thank you," and bowed. When he stood upright, he looked to the young woman and winked.

She stood, curtsied, and sassily declared, "Well, Kora's not here tonight . . . but *I* am."

There was more banging of cups and laughter among the men.

Even Tribb smiled.

Now, the second bard, the older man known as Blaze, stood and walked to the front of the room. He waited for the merriment to subside. Then, with a nod, he acknowledged Tribb, and in a deep, theatrical voice, he began:

> So much for my lusty competitor
> Who would put me out in the rain
> and cold—
> The vociferous young versifier
> Who chants about our lust for gold
> And his lust for an exotic
> paramour.
> He—in simple, repetitive couplets—

Tells us what we know—and
nothing more—
As though he were reciting the
alphabet.

Although most of the crowd did not know the alphabet themselves, they applauded the bard's challenge.

Warmed by the blanket and wine, Tribb was beginning to relax.

Blaze waited for his audience to settle, and then he continued:

Artama, many times, has told the
tale
Of his second return across The
Plain,
And he has spoken in vivid detail
Of the storm—as fierce as a
hurricane—
When the merciless wind blew
everywhere
With screeching, burning,
smothering power,
Blinding him, as the dust filled the

air,
Obliterating sight of the Towers.
His hope was cruelly overtaken
By doubt, and he screamed, but all
he could hear
Was the wind. He felt lost and
forsaken—
Suffocating in regret and blind fear.
The room was hushed.
Eventually, the storm passed, and
he
Was able to progress across The
Plain,
He was able to complete his journey
And return to The Town once again.
The people began to stir.
But there's more to tell about his
return:
Artama is keeping a great secret!
Listen, and I will tell you what I
learned
About it from men I recently met.
The crowd quieted again.

Not long ago, on a night much like
	tonight,
I talked with two worn-out knaves
	in an inn,
And although both are certainly
	downright
Disreputable—one fat and one
	thin—
Both swear their tale is absolutely
	true.
As their tongues loosened with
	more and more drink,
I was quite happy—from my point of
	view—
To buy more and push them over
	the brink.
There were chuckles of appreciation.
	Now, neither was shy about saying
	they
Were bent upon relieving a traveler
Of his burdens and sending him
	away—
Such is the outcome they like and

prefer.

But when they asked what he was
carrying,

He quite simply replied, "Nothing of
yours."

So, the thin bandit drew his sword,
swearing,

"I'll be the judge of that." He was
cocksure.

The crowd laughed, for they knew the
folly of being cocksure.

The traveler drew his weapon from
his scabbard,

And both bandits—unbelieving—
just laughed:

It was only a hilt, not even a dagger,

A joke, an insult to their craft.

But the mounts of both knaves
whinnied and shied.

Although spurred, the horses would
not advance,

Rather, they became too unruly to
ride.

The rogues looked at each other,
   and—with a glance—
Each man indignantly dismounted,
And they began to circle their prey.
The booty was already counted:
This would be child's play.
The audience was now leaning forward.
   The bandits attacked, slashing
      viciously,
   But their quarry quite skillfully
      parried.
   Blades cracked together most
      furiously,
   But according to their commentary,
   They only made one glancing strike
      before
   Both were quickly, efficiently
      disarmed.
   The knaves hopelessly abandoned
      their swords
   In the dust and scrambled away
      unharmed.
Blaze paused.

> Now, they swear the swordsman
>   was Artama,
> And his sword was an *invisible*
>   blade.

Tribb leaned forward.

>   And, so, in conclusion of our
>   drama,
>   They say—without an army to give
>   aid—
>   Artama could have easily killed
>   them
>   With his weapon of invisible heat.
>   More skillful than any of The
>   Kingsmen,
>   He could slice them all to
>   mincemeat.

The bard looked at Tribb, smiled, and bowed with a flourish of his right arm.

At the word "mincemeat," most of the drunken men jumped to their feet and cheered.

Tribb was on his feet, too, the blanket falling from his shoulders. He took a deep breath . . . .

Canter ran from where he was positioned by the front door to where Blaze was standing. He spread his arms as though he were about to embrace the crowd and said, "What a wonderful fantasy! What a delightful imagination! And judging by the noise of this crowd, I declare Blaze to be the winner!"

The crowd cheered.

As the serving wenches moved among the revelers, Canter motioned for one of them to come to him. "Quickly, take the Kingsman a fresh flagon. And he is not to be charged, of course. Go!"

Blaze addressed his audience.

And, so, my friends, in closing, let
me say:
I thank you all for shelter from the
storm

And a meal with my lady at a table.

He winked and nodded toward the young woman who would be Kora for the night.

Thank you all for allowing us to stay

In a comfortable room—cozy and warm.

Blaze nodded toward the young bard.

Or she could sleep with him in the stable.

Everyone knew where she would be spending the night.

Bearing a flagon of mulled wine, the serving wench spoke to Tribb. He chuckled and took his seat as she filled his cup and set the flagon on the tabletop. Then, she took the blanket from the floor and carefully draped it across his shoulders.

Tribb was pondering the bard's tale. Could any of it possibly be true? Could damnable Artama possibly have such a weapon? If he did, Tribb intended to find it.

Tribb intended to wield it.

__IN ALL OF SPACE AND TIME__, in the time and space of E3, liquid water is essential to life . . . as it is known.

Likewise, liquid water is essential on E2 and E1.

Elsewhere, other solvents may sustain other biochemistries.

Among countless and apparently miraculous conditions, each of these worlds orbits a star within a circumstellar habitable zone—not common, but not unknown.

Did water accrete as the planets cooled? Or was it delivered by comets and meteoroids?

8

COVERED IN THE DUST OF DESOLATION, the prisoner's wagon—the black box—rolled through the main gate into Eastedge. Tribb led the way. Two other horsemen trailed him, one on either side of the wagon.

People stopped and stared.

At a command from Tribb, the wagon was turned and brought to a halt (where the puppet show had been), the door facing the people walking to and from the market.

The curious began to gather. They talked with one another nervously. Men, women, and children all knew the black box meant trouble.

Cressa was on her way home, carrying a basket of vegetables.

Several Kingsmen emerged from the headquarters, mounted their horses and rode the short distance to the prisoner's wagon, encircling it, arrogantly glaring, challenging anyone who walked by or stopped.

Nonetheless, an uneasy crowd began to grow.

In the black box, in the feculent straw, Korbin roused from his nightmare, the endlessly recurring recollections of his torture, the pain, and the stench of the gloved Kingsman driving the glowing rod deep into his face—again and again. His eyes were dull, almost lifeless. What was once his face was now an outrage of infected wounds and horrid scars.

Tribb waited impatiently, looking from side to side, as the murmuring crowd increased.

Cressa came upon the assemblage and stopped.

Tribb saw her and grinned, a snarling dog.

Cressa glared in return—with the full hatred of an adult—remembering the dagger at her throat and the sound of the raging river.

In a loud voice, Tribb commanded: "Subjects of D'anor, residents of Eastedge, hear me!"

The murmuring decreased.

Tribb waited for quiet. "Our King has been generous, especially to Eastedge. He has caused the wall to be built, protecting you from those who would plunder. You no longer have need of swords—or other weapons. The King has been unsparing with d'anors, bringing prosperity. Yet there are those among you who do not appreciate D'anor's grace, who would resist his will and his commands." Tribb studied the faces in the crowd. "In fact, there are those—even some in this crowd—who have attempted to organize against him. You should know that such efforts are futile, and they will not be tolerated. They will be crushed." Tribb reined his horse back and forth in the space between the prisoner's wagon and the people.

"As most of you know, there was one utterly foolish young man—Korbin—who spawned the supposedly secret organization known as The Hope of The Radiant Star."

The assembled began to mutter.

"You may have wondered what became of Korbin." Tribb guided his horse to the back of the prisoner's wagon. He motioned to another Kingsman, who dismounted and strode quickly to the door. "Korbin has been a guest in The Capital, and—with some persuasion—he has told us, in great detail, about The Hope of The Radiant Star . . . and those who are involved with it," Tribb lied.

The Kingsman at the door of the black box detached a ring of keys from his belt, selected one, unlocked the padlock, and opened the door.

The people moved about and stretched their necks to see.

The Kingsman reached inside, grabbed Korbin by his hair, and dragged him out of the wagon, dumping him on the ground. Still holding him by the hair, the soldier lifted Korbin's head for the crowd to behold.

Korbin had no face.

The crowd gasped.

There were shrieks.

And sobs.

A woman collapsed and vomited.

Several men stepped forward.

The Kingsmen moved their horses toward the crowd and drew their swords.

Tribb shouted, "*There* is your Korbin! *There* is your Hope of The Radiant Star!"

Cressa was weeping, and she was not alone.

Tribb scowled at the crowd, daring anyone to speak, daring anyone to take another step forward.

Through her tears, Cressa could see Tribb's belligerent smirk. She wiped her eyes with her free hand, and—still carrying her basket—she began walking slowly through the crowd, toward the crumpled, faceless man.

People stepped back, clearing a path.

Some people spoke.

"Be careful."

"Do not get involved."

"Let it be."

"What will your parents say?"

"Stop."

Cressa emerged from the crowd and continued walking—without hesitation—until she reached Korbin. She set her basket on the ground and knelt close to the defaced wretch. Korbin tried to rise, eyes wild. Cressa bent forward and embraced his head, lowering it gently, holding it against her thighs.

Someone called out, "Bless you, girl."

Cressa whispered to Korbin.

From the crowd, "Someone help her."

Tribb scowled.

No one moved.

Cressa stood, and with her help, Korbin began a struggle to stand. He swayed and leaned against her. She worked to hold him steady.

A boy about Cressa's age made his way through the crowd. When he reached the front, after hesitating a moment, he walked to Korbin and helped support him.

The people applauded.

Cressa and the boy began leading Korbin away.

The boy said something to Cressa, and they stopped. He retrieved her basket and returned.

Korbin put an arm around the boy's shoulders, and—with his other arm around Cressa—the three of them shambled away, the boy carrying the basket.

Tribb glowered, memorizing the faces in the crowd. The applause dwindled. Tribb shouted to The Kingsman driving the prisoner's wagon, "Begone!" Immediately, the driver snapped the reins, and the wagon moved away toward the gate, the unlocked door flapping. The two horsemen who had arrived with the wagon rode away with it. Tribb and the remaining Kingsmen rode through the crowd to the headquarters. The people began to straggle away. A few stayed and talked in small clusters. Most headed for home.

The sun was lowering, shadows lengthening.

The empty wagon rattled through the gate into the dust and desolation.

+++++

Cressa, Korbin, and the boy arrived at Cressa's home. She opened the door. Her mother, who had her back to them, was at a table slicing onions. "Dear, where have you been? I need to add the vegetables to the stew."

"Mother, it is horrible."

Cressa's mother turned, saw the horror, and gasped. "What is . . . this?"

"Mother, this is Korbin, the man you and father have been talking about."

"What . . . ?" The woman was speechless.

The boy said, "I must go. My parents will be worried."

"Mother, we must help him."

Gathering her composure, Cressa's mother said, "Take him to the bedroom."

Cressa and the boy helped Korbin, Cressa's mother following, and the three of them helped Korbin onto the bed.

Cressa's mother turned to the boy. "What is your name?"

"Hadee, ma'am."

"Hadee, do you know my husband's shop—Jaspon, the toolmaker?"

"Yes, ma'am."

"Run to him. Tell him to come here immediately. Will you do that?"

"Yes, ma'am."

"Then, run home."

"Yes, ma'am." The boy looked to Cressa, tears in his eyes.

Cressa tried to smile.

Hadee raised his hand and rubbed his forehead, managing his own uncertain smile. He turned and ran out of the cottage.

Korbin moaned.

Cressa's mother urgently instructed her daughter, "Fetch water for him."

Korbin's lips—what remained of them—were dried and split. He was trying to speak. Cressa's mother leaned close to hear, but she could not understand.

Cressa returned and poured some water from a pitcher into a cup. Bubbles appeared for a moment, tended to gather and merge . . . . While her mother raised Korbin's head, Cressa held the cup to his lips. He slurped voraciously. He raised his hand to the cup, tipping it, trying to gulp more, but most spilled down his chin.

Cressa's mother softly admonished, "Slowly. We have all you need."

Jaspon entered the room, "Lana?" He walked to his wife.

She turned. "Cressa says this is Korbin."

"It is, Father. I was coming home from the market. The Kingsman . . . Tribb . . . was displaying him . . . telling everyone *this* is what became of him."

Jaspon clawed his beard. "Damn Tribb. Damn D'anor."

Korbin mumbled something.

Jaspon stepped closer. "What did he say?"

His wife shook her head, unknowing.

Jaspon leaned close to Korbin's ruined face and put his ear to the ravaged lips.

Korbin gathered himself and uttered, "Art . . . a . . . ma."

Jaspon said, "I will go for him. I will bring him back."

Lana hugged her husband and said, "Jaspon . . . be careful."

He kissed her. "I will be back—with Artama."

+++++

In the candlelight, Artama sat alone at the bedside, listening to Korbin struggle for breath. *How could anyone do this? Such twisted hatefulness. How can this be forgiven?*

Artama took a jar from his pocket and removed the lid, the golden glow reminding him: *I used this ointment to heal my wound from the bandit's sword. The voices, the pure voices, the chorus. The harmony resonated and reverberated. Floated far away from the pain. Could see the colors of the chorus and the song everlasting—the blue and gold and white. Radiant healing.* He lightly touched the golden ointment with his fingers. *All of this because of me. All of this anguish flows from my decision to cross The Plain. My decision . . . the result of an endless flow of inscrutable events—each as much the cause of his fate as my decision—yet this is all because of me.* Ever so gently, Artama began applying the golden ointment to Korbin's wounds and scars.

When he finished embrocating the damaged tissue, Artama replaced the lid and returned the jar to his pocket. He placed his open hand on the wreckage of Korbin's face . . . and he prayed.

Somewhere, one by one, cocoons opened and weebon trees glowed in the aura of the metamorphoses. Golden butterflies lifted, fluttering away into the night.

For a moment, Korbin stirred, opened his eyes, and looked deep into the eyes of Artama. He tried to speak but uttered only, "Hhh . . . ." Korbin reached for Artama's hand. Again, he tried to speak—only to exhale his last breath.

DOES LIFE ARISE on the planet from non-living matter—or does life only arise from life? Abiogenesis—or biogenesis? Planetary origins—or extraplanetary?

The moon, still close to the planet, causes extreme tides—washing life onto land.

Ferocious winds churn and disperse the spume.

And the accumulation of atmospheric oxygen allows the formation of an ozone layer, protecting the new life on land.

9

ARTAMA AND HIS FATHER were seated before the fireplace, thankful for the warmth, grateful for the moments of peace. Flames licked around the logs, radiating a comforting golden glow, and—now and then—sparks snapped, jumping and falling to the hearth.

There was a long silence in their conversation. The chairs of both men were drawn near the fire. Artama's legs were extended, his feet very close to the flames. Alagon's feet were pulled close to him, covered by a blanket draped across his lap and legs. He also had a blanket across his shoulders.

Artama was thinking about the night he spent among the spires on The Plain on his second return from E1. *I had a small fire, and close to the flames, absorbing the warmth, in the golden light, I opened the jar Kora had packed. Applied the golden ointment, smoothing it over my wound, the one strike made by the bandits. Closed my eyes, felt the radiant healing, and I heard the pure voices, the chorus.*

On the mantel, a candle burned, honoring Korbin.

The ointment may have restored his face.

Alagon spoke, "You have done all you could, my son. You have done more than anyone could ask." Alagon tightened the blanket around his shoulders.

Artama studied the candle flame—*a constant in our worlds*—thinking of Kora.

Alagon continued, "Now, it is up to the people—each person, individually. As you have often said, the ultimate freedom cannot be achieved by force. Even with the explosives you have described, even if The Kingsmen and D'anor could be defeated, true freedom—Enlightenment—would remain elusive."

Artama shifted in his chair, drawing his feet back from the fire. He looked to the

meteoron hanging on the wall . . . .
remembering Kora singing:

>*I came for you,*
>
>*I came for anyone in pain,*
>
>*And you know I return,*
>
>*And you know I remain.*

Artama touched the talisman on the gold chain around his neck. He closed his eyes, certain he was hearing Kora: *"I love him . . . . I want to be with him. I want to save him."* And he knew.

With painful difficulty, Alagon adjusted himself in his chair. "You should go back."

Artama responded, "I came for you. And I will remain."

"A father should not witness the death of his son, and—although my time is not long—if you persist, you too will be defaced and killed . . . before my time. Go back to E1. Go back to Kora."

A spark snapped and jumped from the fire.

Artama said, "Father . . . Kora is coming *here.*"

There was banging on the door.

Artama sighed heavily, stood, and—after a moment—started for the door.

More banging.

Artama called, "Who is it?"

"Kingsman Tribb! Open the door!"

"What is your purpose?"

"What does it matter? Open the door—or we will break it down!"

Artama looked to his father.

Alagon shrugged and said, "What can be done? It will be."

Artama opened the door, and the night chill blew into the cottage.

Tribb and four other Kingsmen stood waiting in their blood-red capotes. Each of the soldiers, except Tribb, held a lantern. Artama stepped back as Tribb strode inside, followed by the others, shadows lurching in the lantern light.

Artama said, "What is this . . . this trespass?"

Tribb tugged at the cuffs of his black leather gloves. "I think you are hiding something . . . something I want."

Artama's thoughts were boiling. *The writings are not here. They are safe at The Hall . . . in the wine cellar.* The key to the chest where Artama secured them weighed heavily in his pocket. *Even these brutes are not comfortable with challenging the elders and violating The Hall.* And Artama said, "I have nothing of yours."

"I have reason to believe you have a weapon, a sword—an extraordinary sword."

The Crystal. How could he know? Only my father and I know.

Tribb was looking around the room, cold eyes darting from point to point.

The bandits. The bandits were the only ones.

Tribb moved toward the fireplace.

Could he possibly have happened upon those highwaymen . . . arresting them for some assault, some robbery, perhaps?

Tribb motioned toward the candle on the mantel. "Why waste a candle in the firelight?"

Artama answered, "Sadly, you would not understand."

Alagon struggled to his feet and moved between Tribb and the fire.

"Out of my way, old man."

"Speak to my father with respect."

"Why? He is clearly nothing but a dead man walking."

Artama stepped toward Tribb.

Two soldiers stepped toward Artama.

As a diversion, Alagon took the candlestick from the mantel and—cupping his hand to protect the flame—walked slowly to the reading table. With trembling hands, he carefully set the candlestick next to a book.

"And what is this you read?" Tribb snorted.

"Poetry," Artama answered.

Tribb and the other soldiers burst into laughter.

"Poetry?" Tribb scoffed. "And what good is that?"

"Again, all too sadly, you would not understand." Artama shuddered. *Writings scattered across the dust, blowing away in the wind.*

Tribb knew if he controlled the sword with the invisible blade, he could be The Commander General—with a seat on The Council. Again, he saw himself in The Palace, in a splendidly imposing uniform, eating exquisite food, and drinking fine wine from a golden goblet. Officers saluted him. Beautiful women were at his command.

As a further diversion, Alagon said, "The candle honors Korbin."

With his gloved hand, Tribb snuffed out the flame. "Now, that is the end of it." He grinned. "Extinguished. The end of Korbin. The end of The Hope of The Radiant Star."

"In reality," Artama said, "his light will shine forever."

Tribb looked through the archway separating the private space from the production shop. It was dark inside.

"In there, what is it?"

"Our workshop. We make pottery."

"I know what you do." Tribb motioned The Kingsmen toward the shop and commanded, "Find the sword," and The Kingsmen, bearing their lanterns, tramped through the archway. They looked in cabinets and under tables and, in the process, knocked a splendid vase to the floor, where it broke into ruin.

Tribb lingered in the living area, looking around the room. "If you had something to hide—and I know you have *much* to hide—you would hide it well. It may not be here." His eyes fell upon the cabinet by the archway. He shouted, "Two of you, get back in here!"

Two soldiers dashed into the room.

"Move that cabinet out from the wall!"

They did. "Nothing, Sir."

"It may not be here," Tribb said, "but I will be watching."

Artama said, "You are a slave."

"I am a Kingsman."

"You are a slave to your foolish ambition."

Tribb opened the cabinet doors, and—with a sweep of his right hand—he raked across a shelf of jars, spilling the glazing powders onto the floor. "Someday, I will have the opportunity to kill you, and I intend to enjoy it. Until then, praise D'anor."

What is a man to do—faced with such brutal ignorance? At the Academy, The Master of Swordsmanship told me, "You will need these skills in fights for your life. The time is coming, as surely as the sunrise, when you will no longer be able to win by your cleverness alone." Artama felt the heat flush his face. I could make explosives. But, in the end, nothing would change. On the other hand, an era would be established—an era upon which to reflect—

an era to inspire. At last, Artama responded, "Until the day your opportunity arrives, may peace be with you."

"Let's go!" Tribb commanded, and he led the soldiers out of the cottage into the dark chill of the night.

THE HAZY ATMOSPHERE *begins with vapors from volcanoes: hydrogen, helium, methane, carbon dioxide.*

As the atmosphere develops, life develops. Living things change the atmosphere, and those changes, in turn, alter life.

Hydrogen and helium rise and drift away into space.

Oxygen remains—most dissolving into the oceans.

Living on energy from the sun and carbon dioxide from the water, photosynthetic life develops—producing more oxygen, and more oxygen accumulates in the air.

One day the sky turns blue.

10

KORA WAS SAVORING every moment of a hot shower—in all of space and time—a delightful, intimate pleasure. Tomorrow, she would depart—transport to E3. There would be no more hot showers. Kora rinsed away the shampoo lather and let the hot water massage the back of her neck (just above the seventh cervical vertebra, on the tattoo of the symbol of infinity, the lemniscate). In complicated anticipation, Kora was thinking of Artama.

+++++

On E3, wrapped in the fur of a Firebear, in his chair before the fireplace—in all of space and time—Artama was alone, concerned about his father. Alagon's chair was empty—he had gone to his bed, not feeling well. Artama understood medical formulations, but his resources were limited—an abundance of knowledge but a dearth of ingredients, a paucity of chemicals. *Medically, there is no remedy for mortality. At the limit of our understanding, we pray.*

+++++

Kora stood tall before the mirror wall, drying her hair with a towel, admiring herself: She was in the best physical condition of her life. She tossed the towel onto the counter, next to a glass of wine and a plate of chocolate chunks. Kora shook her head, and her lustrous black hair fell across her shoulders, down to her waist. As a result of her training, Kora's biceps and triceps were gracefully, artistically defined—as were the muscles of her abdomen. Her thighs were shapely and strong. Her . . . *derriere* . . . rounded and firm—inviting. Light played across the horizons—the sunrise across the wondrous divide. She knew Artama would be pleased.

Kora squared her shoulders, ran her hands (long fingers with manicured, burgundy-painted fingernails) over the roundness of her breasts and down her abdomen to the front of her hips. She raised to her toes and made a slow pirouette.

She took the glass of wine from the counter and drank fully. She took a bite of chocolate . . . allowing the richness to dissolve slowly in her mouth.

+++++

The Firebear fur was a gift from a pilgrim. Rarely seen, Firebears haunted the far side of The Dragon Mountain. Their fur was red and gold, thick and sumptuous.

Artama gazed into the flames in the fireplace, wishing Kora were wrapped in the fur with him. On the table beside his chair, next to a cup of wine, a plate held a small piece of chocolate—the last of what Kora had given him. Artama did not hesitate. He drank the wine and ate the chocolate.

+++++

Kora's costume was laid out. She would appear dressed in the style of Eastedge, not to appear unnecessarily alien. There would be enough trouble.

She turned off the lights—but let a candle burn—and slid into bed. Tonight would be the last night she would sleep alone.

+++++

Artama stood and stepped closer to the fire, savoring the heat. In time, he kneeled and spread the Firebear fur on the floor. Standing, he walked to the wall where the meteoron hung, took it, returned to his chair, and began to play, singing:

> In the cold
>
> Out there tonight,
>
> A man would need more than gold.
>
> The door is locked.
>
> The drapes are closed,
>
> And I'm here alone with you,
>
> In the golden light—
>
> In front of the fire—
>
> On the fur on the floor.
>
> Your lips are wet with wine,
>
> And you are mine,
>
> My firelight lady.
>
> You are mine,

My firelight lady.

When I see you,
I want you,
And I forget . . . all my troubles.
When I hold you,
I love you,
And I remember . . .
I remember . . .
The golden light—
In front of the fire—
On the fur on the floor.
Your lips are wet with wine,
And you are mine,
My firelight lady.
You are mine,
My firelight lady.

A string broke. Artama stopped playing. *It is time.*

+++++

Kora was floating to sleep when she felt the string break. She slid out of bed, went to a cabinet, took a packet of meteoron strings, put the packet in her pack, and slid back into bed.

+++++

In the indigo sky, the sun was rising—red and gold. Artama was walking to the stable. After the night winds, there was only a slight breeze. The air was cool and fresh.

Inside the stable, a boy was mucking stalls. Artama was of no interest to him.

From a chest on the floor beneath the hanging tack, Artama removed the provisions he had assembled, and he began packing saddlebags. The journey would take three days each way. The Plain would be hot by day and cold by night. Methodically, Artama harnessed and saddled two horses—one he would ride, the other was for Kora. On the trip to the watchtower, Kora's horse would carry most of the burdens: blankets, water, food, rope . . . . Artama slid The Crystal into the horse-mounted scabbard and positioned a blanket over it. *No one will notice. If they do, I will surely need it.*

When Artama rode through the gate, the sun was well above the horizon. *Clear sky, white light, pastel dust—a fine day for a journey.*

The Kingsmen on the ground—and the guards in the towers—all watched Artama as he rode east onto The Plain, but they displayed no concern.

I will soon make this journey again.

+++++

In the morning, dressed in her costume, Kora walked through the entrance of The Transport Center. Although there was no ceremony, there were procedures, and her father, as The Headmaster, was there to witness.

He hugged his daughter and said, "Be ever-vigilant. And, when it is time, bring him back. Artama has other service to render."

"I love you, Father. Thank you."

"I love you. Godspeed."

+++++

On the first night—in the clear, black expanse—Artama admired the stars. The dragon moon was bright—and in two nights would be full. Artama felt for the talisman on the gold chain at his chest. In the cold, he could see his breath. He moved closer to the fire and tightened the blanket around his shoulders.

+++++

Kora heard the pure voices of the chorus. The harmony resonated and reverberated. She had no sense of time. She felt far away from everything—everything except the voices. They were near . . . and inside. She could hear the colors of the song everlasting, beyond the blue and gold and white.

+++++

On the second day, Artama watered the horses at a shallow runnel and refilled his canteen. The horses drank slowly and deeply. The sunlight glinted from the rivulet, reminding Artama of the first time he saw Kora on E1. *At the golden fountain, the water was silver in the sunlight.*

+++++

It was quiet now. Nothing was ever more quiet: the quiet of the moment before consciousness. In the silence absolute, in a shudder of cognizance—a frisson—Kora was *experiencing* Artama. He was on his second journey, leading the unholy horde away from The Town. He was trying to climb the watchtower, struggling to climb beyond the rocks thrown by the guards—climbing for his life. A rock hit his right hand, almost costing him his grip. And then, in a cosmic moment, just when Artama turned his head, a rock hit, splitting open the center of his forehead—a bursting red star of torn flesh—sending blood swirling in the air— the birth of The Radiant Star. Artama could only endure. Beyond that, he was helpless. But if he endured, he could climb beyond the threat of the rocks, beyond the power of the guards.

+++++

On the second night, Artama dreamed of Kora—her long, black hair and deep, dark, eternal eyes. Her graceful curves. She wore gold hoop earrings . . . and the golden chain and pendant—the talisman—the gold coin struck with the image of a dragon.

Artama awoke. In the cold light of the dragon moon, he felt terribly alone . . . far away . . . far away from everything. Lying on his back, he watched the dragon move slowly across the sky.

+++++

Kora apperceived Artama reaching the top of the watchtower. He crawled over the wall of rocks on the rim. On the other side, exhausted, he leaned back against the rocks, blood running down his nose and cheeks. Kora felt Artama's fear . . . and pain . . . and relief. Finally, he was safe . . . for the moment . . . .

+++++

On the third day, Artama arrived at the watchtower. Before dismounting, he looked up to the top—a long climb. He remembered the first time, not knowing what he would do, knowing only that he must do *something* to escape Zortan and his beastly men.

Today, his heart was pounding in anticipation of seeing Kora. Now, he knew what to expect—what to do—how to make the climb. He dismounted, took a heavy coil of rope, and began. He would secure the rope at the top. Today, he would use it to lift provisions. Tomorrow . . . .

+++++

Kora envisioned Artama's writings blowing away in the wind, scattering across the dust . . . and the indistinguishable figure riding away madly.

Kora felt Artama's rage.

+++++

On top of the watchtower, Artama wrapped himself in his blanket and leaned against the low stone wall. *Like the wall around Kora's pool.* In the sunset golden light, the cold night approaching, the heat from the wall was welcome. Surrounded by the desolation of The Plain, in the middle of eternity, in the center of infinity, Artama watched a dusty golden spider weave a web between two rocks, running splendid spokes and then adding concentric polygons . . . miraculous and common . . . spectacular and mundane.

Then, Artama heard the unmistakable sound: Flying toward him came three dragons—light and quick—with searching, bright, red eyes. Artama laughed, remembering the terror of the first time. Now, one of the dragons flew straight toward him. Their eyes met. A current of joy coursed Artama's spine. In salutation, he raised his right hand. The dragon rolled . . . and rolled again . . . spiraling over Artama and flying away.

In time, it grew dark, and Artama studied the heavens—waiting. He thought he glimpsed something . . . and was instantly blinded by an unimaginable flash of light.

Artama had experienced the transport—the journey and the arrival—four times, but he had never *witnessed* one: the colors of the chorus, the pure voices, the song everlasting, beyond the blue and gold and white.

When Artama recovered his sight, he saw the most wonderful sight of his life—Kora. Translucent, gossamer. Dark eyes radiantly ethereal. Dark hair floating in stardust.

She smiled.

Artama was no longer cold. He was warm—a sense of well-being unknown since the pool.

He walked toward the shimmering vision, and she walked toward him.

He opened his arms, and she stepped in.

Everything was flowing crystal at the edge. There was no time. They were safe . . . in the moment . . . in the middle of eternity . . . floating together in the center of infinity. Immortal.

As one, they said, "I love you."

__THE STAR HEATS THE ATMOSPHERE__ of the planet, more at the equator, less at the poles, and the resulting difference in atmospheric pressure—the warmer gases rising and the cooler gases moving to replace them—generates the wind.

The rotation of the planet deflects the movement—the macro direction being the result of the balance between the Coriolis force and the pressure gradient force.

At the surface level, the topography, the landscape, alters the flow, and the flow, abrading, alters the landscape.

11

IT WAS THE DAY OF THE WEDDING, and Eastedge was vibrant with joy.

Even though Kingsmen were everywhere.

The original thought was to have a simple, small ceremony: Artama, Kora, Alagon, The Readers, friends, and neighbors. But with the news that Artama and Kora were to be wed—and with the news that Valdar, a former Reader, would perform the ceremony—hope blossomed, lives changed, journeys began.

Such a wedding was an outrage to D'anor. Marriages could only be sanctified by priests of Nam. But the travel ban was too late. Hundreds of people had already arrived in Eastedge. All the rooms at the public-house were quickly taken, as were the rooms at The Berry. Many travelers were housed by residents, and many tents were erected outside the wall.

Wagons of weebon wine arrived at the public-house and The Berry.

+++++

D'anor was furious, shouting at the members of The Council. "How can this happen?! Damned Artama is marrying . . . some whore . . . from another world . . . in a ceremony in Eastedge?! I have banned travel to that cursed town, and yet there is a pilgrimage?!"

In his defense, The Commander General said, "My Lord, the pilgrimage was underway before you made your decree. The people were already moving. The timing of such an onslaught is beyond our resources."

"I am The King by divine right from Nam. And you tell me . . . the *timing* . . . is beyond our resources?!"

The High Priest spoke, "We do not always understand the ways of Nam."

D'anor was about to respond harshly, but The Jester was at his side, whispering in his ear. The King nodded, and The Jester returned to his seat. At last, D'anor spoke: "As much as I would like to crush this outrage in Eastedge, I will not. To do so would require complete slaughter." D'anor glared at The Commander General and added, "Because of our currently inadequate resources in the region—and because I will do nothing to make Artama a martyr—I will take another approach: disappearances and defacements."

+++++

Between the gate and the headquarters of The Kingsmen—on the spot of the puppet show— where Korbin was dumped—carpenters had built a platform, a stage for the ceremony.

The sun was lowering, casting a golden glow upon those gathered.

The platform was built to the height of two men, a stage large enough for three people. Ascending to the platform were three staircases: one for Valdar, one for Artama, and one for Kora. Valdar's stairway was at the back of the structure. Kora's was closest to the main gate, and Artama's was opposite, closest to the headquarters. Each flight of stairs had a railing, and there was also a railing around the stage, open only at each staircase. Covering the floor was an exquisitely woven rug of the deepest blue—displaying a golden sun and silver stars. Above the stage, banners—azure, gold, and white—fluttered in the breeze.

The gold of the sunset became increasingly red.

This was Tribb's opportunity: Artama was living on the edge—anything could require the use of force. Tribb needed to be in the right place at the right time. Now, he was on the wall, near the tower at the main gate, pacing along the battlements. From his vantage point, he could see everything.

The occupying platoon commander—a lieutenant—stood nearby.

To the frustration of Tribb, the lieutenant was in command.

Tribb found Cressa in the crowd, and he began watching her jealously.

Everyone had a different reason, but everyone knew this was a momentous occasion. Many thought this could be the beginning of a new era. Some were seekers of Enlightenment. Others were simply curious—or only looking for fun. Most needed something to celebrate.

Tribb was bitter: He could force a confrontation, but the lieutenant was interested in maintaining peaceful order.

Hape was among the crowd, standing near the headquarters. He could see Tribb on the wall. Hape was tormented, living on the edge of winning The King's favor or being outdone by Tribb.

Alagon was witnessing the culmination of his life. Once, he had been married to a beautiful, wondrous woman. Once, he had been blind, unable to see his newborn son. In time, his son traveled across The Plain and returned with the ointment—miraculously healing his eyes—and, now, he was witnessing the wedding of his son to an angel.

In the crowd, the families of Cressa and Hadee were standing together. Cressa and Hadee were holding hands.

Tribb huffed.

The fat clown moved among the crowd.

Hape watched Tribb on the wall as he passed behind merlons and appeared in crenels.

Tribb was possessed by Cressa.

Hape was anguished: Anything could happen to overwhelm his plan. This wedding would push D'anor to action, with or without him.

Alagon was at peace.

At first unnoticed, Valdar began ascending his staircase. Seeing the golden robe—the golden robe of the former First Reader—people began pointing, and the crowd began to quiet. Valdar slowly, carefully ascended the stairs, stopping once to steady himself. By the time he reached the stage, the throng was hushed.

As Hape thought about it, fortunately, the platoon commander was stifling Tribb. For now.

From the tent near the headquarters, Artama appeared, and, dressed in the color of a cloudless sky, he walked toward the platform.

The assembled began to cheer.

Artama ascended his staircase, two steps at a time.

From the tent near the main gate, Kora appeared, wearing a flowing white gown. She walked gracefully, majestically, toward the scaffolding. The light of the setting sun glinted from her golden necklace and golden hoop earrings.

Again, the crowd hushed.

Kora ascended her staircase with unselfconscious elegance.

In his golden robe, standing before the multitude of witnesses, Valdar pressed together the palms of his hands—in a gesture of supplication—and, in a resounding voice, he spoke: "We are gathered here . . . not to sanctify the marriage of Artama and Kora . . . but to celebrate it!"

A cheer arose.

"For no man—or woman—can sanctify. Most certainly not an ancient man in a golden robe . . . ."

The crowd chuckled.

"No priest."

Quiet.

"No king!"

The crowd cheered.

Valdar waited. "There is no need to sanctify this marriage before the people . . . or a king. For within The One . . . it is."

And the people cheered louder than ever.

Valdar held a small, ornately carved wooden box. Inside the box, nestled in a cushion of fine fabric, were the rings—two rings carved from stone by the artisans of the far western edge of The Kingdom. The rings were astoundingly highly polished, glowingly translucent.

Valdar gave Kora's ring to Artama. "Artama, do you give this ring to Kora—this circle—this symbol of the infinity of Love?"

"I do." Artama slipped the ring onto the index finger of Kora's right hand. The scar—the star—in Artama's forehead glowed.

Valdar turned. He gave Artama's ring to Kora. "Kora, do you give this ring to Artama—this circle—this symbol of the infinity of Love?"

"I do." And Kora slipped the ring onto the index finger of Artama's right hand.

Valdar spoke: "Before the people . . . within The One . . . you are wed."

Now, there was a crescendo of a glorious, victorious cheer. People began to hug and dance.

Hape knew it was time to act—time to work the alliance with Tribb.

Cressa and Hadee kissed.

At the sight, Tribb spit through a crenel. He strode to the top of a staircase and began descending within the wall.

Excitedly, the crowd began to disperse—some toward the public-house—some, eventually, to The Berry—others toward the neighborhoods.

Hape could no longer see Tribb on the wall, and he began making his way toward the main gate. He knew, eventually, Tribb would appear.

The fat clown headed toward the neighborhood celebrations.

+++++

As the light and the warmth of the sun faded, bonfires were started along the streets. Over the frenetic rhythms of drummers, flute players were creating sensual melodies. Bards recounted the tale of Artama. Wineskins were abundant and shared with strangers. Couples were dancing and singing. Even though it was cool, curtains and shutters were open, and light glowed from the windows of every dwelling. Strangers became friends.

Artama and Kora walked through the crowd—smiling and waving. The people

stepped back—clearing a path for the couple—
and shouted heartfelt best wishes.

Golden sparks from the bonfires, the
myriad hopes and dreams of the people,
swirled upward, rising toward the uncountable
silver stars.

In the chill, those not dancing moved
closer to the fires, ate spiced meat and
vegetables wrapped in flatbread, and drank.

Hadee and Cressa were among the
dancers.

Eventually, after making their way
through the crowd, near their home, Artama
and Kora stood talking quietly with their
neighbors.

Nearby, Alagon stood with Valdar (no
longer wearing the golden robe), and the two
old men—the two old friends—spoke to one
another soberly.

Kingsmen stood in the shadows.

Alagon leaned to Valdar and whispered.
Valdar put his hand on his friend's shoulder
and nodded. Alagon then made his way toward

Artama and Kora, and when he reached them, he hugged Kora, then Artama. He spoke quietly to them. Father and son hugged again. Then, Alagon turned and tottered home.

Not long after Alagon departed, Artama and Kora excused themselves, and—holding hands—they too made their way home. When they reached the front door, Artama said, "I want to see that my father is comfortably settled. I will not be long." They hugged and shared a kiss. Then, inside, Artama went to his father's bedroom, and Kora went to theirs.

Outside, the celebration continued, sparks and music and laughter rising into the night.

Alone in the bedroom, Kora lit several candles. She poured wine from a jug into two cups. The jug and cups, each bearing the design seen on the rug on the stage—the golden sun and silver stars—were gifts from Artama's apprentices. Kora removed several chunks of chocolate from a small wooden box she had brought from E1 and arranged them on a plate. She rotated the wedding ring on her finger and smiled. She removed it, held it near a candle flame—admiring the translucent beauty—and slipped it back on her finger.

Kora undressed.

She took a sip of wine. Then another. She set the cup on the table, took a piece of chocolate, drew it sensuously into her mouth, letting it melt slowly, the creamy richness warming her. She ran her hands over her breasts, down across her stomach—feeling the muscles of her abdomen—and down across the front of her hips. Yes, Artama would be pleased. She slipped into a burgundy silk robe and lay on the bed—fragrant from her afternoon bath.

Especially for this occasion, Artama had built a wooden bathtub for Kora. Water was carried from the river, heated in kettles, and a few drops of aromatic oil were added. In the bath, Kora remembered floating on her back in the pool on E1. She remembered rolling over and diving below the surface and meeting

Artama's eyes in deep vision—everything flowing crystal at the edge . . . in the moment.

Artama knocked gently on the door to his father's room. There was no response. Again, he knocked—a little louder—and once more, there was no reply. Artama quietly opened the door and looked inside. His father was sleeping peacefully, breathing softly. Artama stood silently watching, with the same contentment a parent feels when watching a child sleeping serenely. Artama closed the door and walked toward the bedroom he and Kora shared.

At the door, Artama knocked softly and then entered, smiling. Kora motioned for him to come to her, and he did, lying beside her. She moved toward him, and they embraced. Artama inhaled deeply, delighting in the intoxicating fragrance of Kora's hair. Eventually, Kora rolled away, stood, walked to the table, and took the cups of wine. She gave one to Artama. They toasted silently and drank. Kora set her cup on the table, took the plate of chocolate, and held it out to Artama. He swung his feet over the side of the bed. He took a piece of chocolate, as did Kora, and with the chocolate, they toasted silently. Kora put her morsel into Artama's mouth, and Artama put his into hers. They allowed the chocolate to melt, then kissed.

Kora stepped back and looked into Artama's eyes. She sighed. After a long pause, Kora said, "We need to return to E1. There is going to be trouble. We need to leave. This wedding . . . this gold—" Kora put a hand to her necklace. "All these people gathering. All this will push D'anor to action."

"True."

Kora continued, "We know Tribb will use any excuse to harm you . . . to kill you. Hape is deceitful and ambitious. Your writings are at risk. Visioning, I have seen Hape stealing them. D'anor will have us defaced . . . and worse. And the fate of your father . . . is unthinkable."

"I know . . . and that is why I cannot leave . . . as long as my father lives. He would be at the mercy of Tribb . . . and his Kingsmen."

Kora sighed again.

Artama continued, "Our presence creates this trouble, but our presence also restrains D'anor." Artama reached for Kora's hand, drawing her to the bed. "If I attempt to remove the writings from The Hall, Hape will notice. What he would do then, I do not know."

Kora sat beside Artama. She put her hand on his thigh.

Artama said, "And there is much more to be done here."

Kora almost sobbed.

Artama kissed her gently on the forehead, and then he stood. "But these are concerns for tomorrow—another day. Tonight, we celebrate!" He walked to where the meteoron was hanging on the wall, took it down, returned to the bed, and sat beside Kora again. Softly, he began to play, and gradually, the strings began to glow in blue and gold and white.

Tears welled in Kora's eyes.

Artama played with increasing passion and began to sing:

> The first time I saw you,
>
> I saw you open the door.
>
> I knew you were the one—
>
> The one I was looking for.
>
> I knew you were the one—
>
> The one I was praying for.
>
> I knew you were the one . . .
>
> And you are so much more.
>
> Now, you are the one—
>
> The one I adore.
>
> You are the one,
>
> And you are so much more.

> I love you in the morning.
>
> All day, you beguile.
>
> At night, I love the candlelight of
>
> Your enchanting smile.

You are a miracle—destined to be—
The mother of our child,
And you are so much more.

Blue and gold and white
From the moment before
The perfect crystal sunlight began
Shining forevermore,
You seemed to be the light—
The light of love.
You seemed to be the light,
And you are so much more.

Kora kissed Artama on the cheek.

Artama stood, hung the meteoron on the wall.

Kora reclined on the bed.

Artama returned and lay next to her.

They kissed . . . a loving, lingering kiss. Artama kissed Kora's eyes and ears, then nuzzled his face into her hair. Drums and flutes, rhythm and melody. Kissed her lips again . . . wet and soft. In the candlelight, Artama opened Kora's robe and kissed her breasts. She ran her hand down his stomach and beyond . . . began to unbuckle his belt. Artama rolled off the bed, stood, undressed—kicking off his sandals and tossing his clothes on the floor. The star in his forehead pulsed. He took a drink of wine and lay again next to Kora. Wine still wet on his lips, he began kissing the warm firmness of her nipples. Her mouth. Caressing her. Artama was hard and heavy in Kora's hand. Her lips parted, and she softly moaned. Artama rose to his knees, admiring her bright eyes, lustrous hair, hungry mouth. Kora, with a firm grip, guided him inside.

On E1, in the pool, under the water, their eyes met in deep vision. Everything flowing crystal at the edge. Atoms swirling into galaxies and coalescing into stars and planets and moons . . . . Artama saw his earth orbiting his sun, and he saw the dragon moon orbiting his earth. In the moment, in the middle of eternity, there was no time. He was . . . there

. . . now . . . floating in the center of infinity. Immortal.

They rolled over. Kora's golden hoop earrings swinging, golden necklace dangling, as she leaned down to kiss him. Sitting on his pillar of passion, she bounced in a frenzy of joy. Looking into his eyes, she saw the colors of the chorus of pure voices—eternally . . . infinitely . . . now. Immortal.

Kora moved off Artama and rolled onto her stomach, raised to her knees and elbows, and pressed her face into the pillow, turned her head to the side, mouth open. Artama brushed aside her hair, kissed the back of her neck, lingering on the tattoo—the symbol of infinity—the lemniscate. He nuzzled into her hair. And entered her again. Together, they moaned. He raised upright and gripped her shoulders. Kora tossed her head from profile to profile. She extended her arms and pushed against the wall, pushing back hard into Artama. He moved his hands from her shoulders and caressed her breasts, then moving his hands down, he held her at the waist, then the hips. Pumping. Within the blue and gold and white, in a flash of light so bright the galaxy is overwhelmed, neutron stars collide . . . exploding.

UNDER THE HEAT OF THE STAR, on the surface of the planet, from lakes and oceans, liquid water evaporates into the air.

Water vapor, requiring a non-gaseous surface to transition from vapor to liquid, eventually condenses on condensation nuclei.

Droplets fuse to create larger droplets—coalescence. As air turbulence occurs, droplets collide, producing larger droplets. Coalescence continues, and drops become heavy enough to overcome air resistance and fall as rain, returning to the surface—eventually flowing into lakes and oceans.

Potentially to evaporate again.

12

THE LATE-AFTERNOON SUNLIGHT filled Alagon's bedroom with a warm glow. Alagon was in bed, reclining upon several pillows. The sunlight was shining through a window to his right, and he was observing the clouds as they moved slowly across the sky, watching them take on the pink and lavender of the beginning sunset. Although the room was comfortable, he felt cold—even though, earlier, Kora had covered him with an extra blanket. On the left side of the bed was a nightstand. On the tabletop were small bowls of powders (medicines Artama had made), a spoon, and an empty cup.

There was a gentle knock on the door.

"Come in."

Artama and Kora entered, Kora carrying a pitcher of water. She walked to the nightstand and filled the cup—bubbles appeared, tended to gather and merge . . . . She added a spoonful of a vermillion powder, stirred it until it dissolved, and then passed the cup to Alagon. She set the pitcher on the table and seated herself on a chair next to the bed.

Alagon drank eagerly. The vermillion would eventually warm him. It always lifted his spirit.

Artama walked to the opposite side of the bed and sat on a chair with his back to the window.

Alagon reached out to his left—toward the nightstand—with the empty cup, his hand trembling. Kora took the cup and set it on the tabletop. Alagon turned to his son and said, "She is truly beautiful in this light."

Artama smiled. "She is truly beautiful . . . in any light."

Kora blushed. "Is there anything I can do?"

"Thank you, but I think not," said Alagon. "My bones ache, I am cold, and I am tired—very tired. But you have done all you can." A clement breeze moved through the window and across the bed. "I have been dreaming and remembering—remembering my life. The dreams have been wonderful—very pleasant, very comforting. And I have remembered so much from so long ago. Time seems to have vanished."

"As we have spoken in the past," Artama struggled with the limitations of language, "time is an appealing verisimilitude, a useful construct—but an illusion."

Alagon laughed—the cosmic, inscrutable laughter of a man facing death, the ultimate unknown. "And within that illusion, my time is at hand." He adjusted himself on the pillows and continued, "What happens?"

"What do you mean?"

"What happens next—at death?"

"I do not know." Artama shifted in his chair. "I only think I know."

"What do you *think*?"

"Life is eternal. The spirit is eternal. Consciousness is eternal. Energy is eternal. There is no loss of energy or consciousness or spirit or life—only change."

"You speak of bubbles . . . ."

"As a metaphor, as an example of separation from a greater field, the separation of the individual from the field of infinite consciousness . . . from the field of pure potentiality."

Alagon smiled. He knew his son would be eloquent.

Artama continued, "I think we transcend the limits of this spatiotemporal experience . . . we return to The One—Love—the blessed, blissful, all-encompassing understanding . . . ."

Alagon chuckled. "You speak like someone from E1."

Kora smiled. "Truly."

Artama nodded. "Some say we are reincarnated, living through many separations—living through many lives—until we are utimately, cosmically perfected."

"Why the separation?" asked Alagon. "Why imperfection needing to be perfected?"

Artama nodded again. "The eternal question of the separated: Why?"

And Kora said, "Why life?"

Alagon reached for Kora's hand, took it, and squeezed. "I would like to say goodbye to Valdar."

Kora kissed Alagon's hand and said, "I will bring him."

Alagon released her, and Kora left the room, quietly closing the door.

Alagon turned to his son (silhouetted against the sunset aura of the window) and said, "She reminds me so much of your mother—" Alagon paused. Tears came to his eyes. His lips pressed tightly together. His eyes closed. Lips trembled. He took a deep breath, sighed heavily, and continued, "She reminds me so much of . . . Elle. Your mother was beautiful—the envy of every eye. Graceful and gracious and knowing and kind. From the first time I saw Kora, I was reminded of Elle."

I remember her kindness, her warmth . . . her fragrance.

"It is in the eyes. Kora has those same dark, deeply mysterious eyes. And the same dark, lustrous hair. Elle was astoundingly arresting, the desire of every young man. Like Kora, she could look *into* you, into your soul."

"How did you meet?"

"By the river, one morning. She was fetching water. As was I. She was my destiny, I knew. I started a conversation. Her voice was wonderful—music. Feeling bold, I said, 'As beautiful as you are, I cannot believe I have never seen . . . never noticed you before.'"

"And, what happened?"

"She laughed. Said she just arrived. 'From where?' I asked, and she laughed again and said, 'Far away—far, far away.' She was always coy about that—never would be specific. Of course, now I wonder, but back then, I knew nothing of E1.

"She was staying with an elderly couple in town. They both died many years ago."

"She would never say where she was from?"

"No. Always mysterious . . . secretive about that." Alagon shifted on the pillows, "I was so honored by her affection . . . ." He fell silent. "She seemed magical, seemed to understand so much, particularly about healing. She was the person to seek if you were sick. She was like you are now. Kept a garden of herbs and other plants. People brought her seeds. She used the plants to make medicines."

Could she have been? Why not?

"Eventually, we were married. Our wedding was a simple affair—nothing like yours turned out to be." Alagon smiled at the memory. He closed his eyes and was silent.

The aura of the window had changed from pink and lavender to deep gold.

Artama sat silently in anticipation.

Alagon opened his eyes. "In time, Elle was with child, carrying you. We were the happiest couple in The Town. But then . . . I began to lose my sight. Gradually, a film grew over my eyes. Finally, I was blind.

"Elle grew sad. She knew the cure for my blindness but did not have the proper ingredients. What she needed could not be made from the plants she grew. What she needed was far, far away.

"You were born, and it was a joyous occasion. I was a proud father. I never saw you with my eyes—but in my mind, I proudly saw you grow." Alagon fell silent. "I was proud of your reputation as an artist—even as a boy."

"Father, I am proud of *you*. If it were not for you—"

Alagon interrupted, "And then your mother died."

"What happened?"

"She was thrown from a horse. It was the saddest day of my life." Alagon stopped speaking. Tears began to fill his eyes again. "In the late afternoon, she went for a ride—she used to love riding along the river at sunset.

"She was gone too long. I felt something was wrong. I knew it was dark—I could not see, but I *could* sense light. Elle always came home by dark. I went to a neighbor's cottage and asked for help. He rode to the river, saw her horse standing near the edge of the water. There was no rider to be seen. Her horse had its head down as though it were grazing. But then my friend realized the horse was nudging something on the ground. He hurried over and saw it was . . . Elle." Alagon stopped to compose himself. "He brought her body home. I demanded that he tell me everything. He said, when he found her, her face was covered with sand and blood. Her eyes open . . . but not seeing. He spoke to her, but she did not respond. She was not breathing . . . ."

Artama reached for his father's hand.

"He laid her body on this bed . . . this very bed. I lay by her, held her in my arms, and wept. I wept all night." Alagon wept quietly now. After a few moments, he opened his eyes and gazed at the ceiling. He was trying to focus on something far away, something far above him.

Artama looked into his father's eyes, then toward the ceiling. Alagon was focusing on something Artama could not see.

There was a soft knock on the bedroom door. The door opened slowly, and Kora appeared. She walked into the room, followed by Valdar.

"My old friend, please come."

Valdar approached the bedside opposite Artama and took Alagon's left hand.

Artama released his father's right hand and stepped back toward the window. The sky was darkening behind him.

Alagon squeezed Valdar's hand and said, "It is good to see you . . . one last time. I wanted to say farewell."

Kora stood quietly at the foot of the bed.

Valdar said, "I will miss you terribly."

Everyone was silent.

Alagon released Valdar's hand and turned to Artama. "I spoke of destiny . . . . I knew Elle was mine. I have often wondered: Are we free?"

"What do you mean?"

"I mean . . . do we have free will?"

How do I honestly answer? I do not know. Sometimes it appears so. Another verisimilitude? Unenlightened wishful thinking? We are driven by ideas—thoughts. What creates an idea? Whence a thought? A motivation? Artama answered, "Another eternal question. Even with the knowledge of E1 . . . I do not know." Artama looked to Kora.

She smiled.

Artama continued, "I do not think so. If we cannot determine our thoughts—the original ideas, the origins of all that follows—how can we determine our ultimate actions?" He paused. "At the quantum level, it is all beyond our control." He added, "You can will yourself to act, but you cannot will yourself to will." He looked again to Kora.

Tenderly, she spoke, "It makes no difference."

Valdar asked, "What do you mean?"

Kora replied, "We act as though we are. We seem to believe we are."

Valdar asked, "If we are not free, what of moral behavior—recognizing right from wrong?"

Artama rejoined the conversation. "Describing behavior as right or wrong is describing what an enlightened being would do, comparing that with what an unenlightened being would do. A perfect, enlightened being would behave lovingly, in harmony with The One."

Alagon said, "We have rules and codes—even laws. We make judgments."

Artama responded, "Our judgments are the results of incomplete understanding—at their best, attempts to describe what an enlightened being would do. An enlightened being would make no judgments."

Valdar asked, "But what of responsibility for our actions?"

"If we cannot control the birth of a thought, the origin of an idea, the cause of a motivation, how can we be responsible for the result?"

Alagon spoke, "But what of obviously terrible, brutal behavior—like the defacement of Korbin?" He stopped speaking, pressing his lips firmly together.

I wish I knew.

Valdar spoke, "Why pain? Why suffering?"

It always comes to this . . . in the end: Why?

"I can only think of separation, isolation, the absence of the awareness of unity—but why the separation, I do not know. But in the separation, there occurs—there are words for—empathy, benevolence, and charity."

The room was silent.

Finally, Alagon said, "My son, tell me again, what is next?"

"Father, after all my travels and all my experiences—after all my studies and meditations and thoughts—I believe you are returning to the cosmic, unseparated consciousness, to pure consciousness, the essence of unlimited potentiality, the field of endless energy and information—Love."

Alagon smiled. "Pray it is so."

Valdar looked to Artama and said, "We have always been truthful with one another—each of us in this room—and now is clearly a moment of truth." He paused. "Do you think prayer is effective?"

Artama answered, "I pray."

"But do you believe it alters events?"

How do I honestly answer?

"Is my prayer effective? Does it change the course of events? Or is it merely my fervent wish?"

"Precisely," said Valdar. "What do you think?"

"I do not know."

"But what do you *think*?"

"Through the ages, the wise have encouraged prayer, and who am I to disagree?"

"Artama, do you believe it alters events?" Valdar pressed.

"Whenever my prayer begins as a longing for a specific result, it quickly becomes less and less a request for that outcome and more and more the expression of a desire to become accepting of the unfolding events—and the eventual result. As I pray, my prayer becomes a prayer to be in harmony. My personal desire fades. Praying for a specific result seems to be a manifestation of separation—an incomplete understanding."

Alagon looked to Kora and then to Artama. "You have both talked with me at length about the magic and mysteries of life. I do not have the knowledge you have, but I believe you."

The bedroom was growing dark. Kora began lighting candles. Occasionally, air moved gently through the window, causing the candle flames to flutter.

Valdar took Alagon's hand and said, "You have been a great friend to me."

Alagon said, "You have been a great friend to me as well. Peace be with you."

Valdar nodded, released Alagon's hand, and stepped back.

Kora stepped forward and took Alagon's hand. She leaned down and kissed his forehead.

Alagon said, "Thank you for the love you have shown me. Thank you for the love you have shown my son. I know you will cherish him and care for him. Peace be with you." Alagon turned to Artama, took his hand, and squeezed. "My son, you have been a blessing to me . . . and to the people. As it is my time, it is also yours. Leave. Go back. You have shown the way. You have done all you can do. The people will do what they will do. May peace be with you." Alagon closed his eyes, and he smiled. His hands opened, releasing Artama and Kora—releasing himself.

The night winds were not yet stirring. Stars began to appear. The dragon moon was bright as it rose above the horizon.

THE LITHOSPHERE, *the crust and upper mantle of the surface of the planet—the rigid shell—is broken, and the tectonic plates ride the asthenosphere.*

Along convergent boundaries, where plates collide at glacial speed, subduction carries the lower plate down into the mantle, and the upper plate rises, buckling and folding—forming mountains.

Along these boundaries, volcanoes form, erupting—creating more mountains.

The spreading surface splits a plate, and a block drops down relative to its flanking blocks—more mountains.

13

ARTAMA AND KORA were enjoying breakfast: freshly baked bread (delivered warm from the bakery by the baker's son), goat cheese, and fruit. They were sipping wee-cho.

Soft morning light gave the room a golden glow.

Artama said, "You are especially radiant this morning."

Kora smiled but was silent. She sipped from her cup.

Artama leaned back in his chair. "What?"

Kora smiled again and said, "I am to be a mother."

Silently, Artama stood, stepped toward Kora, knelt beside her chair, and embraced her.

Kora hugged him and kissed the radiant star on his forehead.

There was loud knocking on the door.

Nothing good comes in this way. Artama looked into Kora's eyes. Then he looked toward the door. *Blood pooling in the dust and four birds circling.* He shivered.

The knocking continued, even more urgently.

Artama sighed. He stood, went to the door, and opened it.

It was Valdar. "The writings are gone!"

Artama stepped back, motioned for Valdar to come in, and closed the door.

Breathlessly, the elder continued, "I went to The Hall to meet with Hape and Abrok, as we do every morning. I was the first to arrive. The door to the wine cellar was open. Standing at the top of the stairs, I listened. I heard nothing. I called for you, but there was no answer. I went downstairs, straight to the chest. Someone had destroyed the lock. The chest was empty. Your writings were gone. I came upstairs just as Abrok arrived. I told him to find Hape and meet us here."

There was more knocking on the door.

Artama opened it.

Abrok was sweating, breathing heavily. "Hape was not at home. As I made my way here, I stopped people and asked whether they had seen him. Several had. He and Tribb were on horseback, and Hape was leading a packhorse laden with saddlebags and bundles of lapa sheets. They rode out the main gate."

Artama turned to Kora. "The time has come. Do what must be done."

Kora hugged Artama. "I love you," she said.

"I love you."

Critical cosmic moments passed in silence.

At last, Artama spoke: "I must go . . . and stop them."

Kora wanted to say, "Be careful," as she let go, but that time was long past.

Artama embraced her again and kissed her. Then he stepped back, turned, and went to the cabinet where The Crystal was hidden. He pulled the cabinet out from the wall.

Valdar and Abrok watched in silence.

Artama removed the boards from the back of the cabinet and retrieved the scabbard. He drew The Crystal and swung it back and forth, slicing shimmering lemniscates in the air.

Valdar and Abrok watched in awe.

Artama sheathed The Crystal, knowing that, this time, taking the weapon meant he would use it. He reached back and removed the leather satchel. *Blood in the dust. Birds descending.*

At the door, Artama hugged Abrok, then Valdar . . . then Kora. He kissed her goodbye and whispered, "See you on the other side." He turned and went out the doorway.

Artama ran toward the stable. He carried the scabbard in one hand and the satchel in the other.

Any other day, it would have been a wonderful morning. The sky was clear—cerulean. The air was crisp and fresh. *They will be heading for The Capital. Hape and the packhorse will slow them. Kora will be fine. She will be gone before anyone thinks to look for her. May I have the ear of God.* Artama made his last turn at the blacksmith's shop and ran straight to the stable, through the front doorway, through the tack room, and down a short hallway to the stalls. Brax, the owner, was talking with the stable boy, his son Minto. They both turned abruptly when Artama appeared.

"Artama!" Brax shouted.

"I need your help!"

"What is it?"

"In private."

"Minto, go to the bakery. Get two breakfast rolls . . . on my account. Take one to your mother, and eat the other one yourself. Then, come back to the stalls. Go, now!"

Delighted, the boy dashed away.

"Artama, what can I do?"

"I need the best horse you can give me—fast and strong. I need to ride immediately. Kora will be here shortly. She will need another strong, fast horse. You will probably never see these animals again."

"What is the matter? Why the scabbard?"

"It is best that you do not know. I say that as a friend."

"I will give you Lightning. He is my best."

Artama handed the satchel to Brax. "This will more than pay for your horses."

"Artama, I would gladly give you my horses."

Brax opened the satchel and looked inside. It was filled with bundles of d'anors—enough to buy herds of horses. "Artama!"

"Silently, use all you need. Secretly, use the rest to help others."

"But . . . ."

"I will have no use for any of it."

"What . . . ?"

"I must leave."

Artama and Brax worked together, saddling Lightning. At last, Artama attached the scabbard. Without saying a word, Brax walked away and went down the hallway. When he returned, he was carrying a water bag and a blanket. He hung the bag on the saddle horn and draped the blanket over the scabbard. Artama turned, embraced him, and said, "Thank you." Artama mounted Lightning and rode out of the stable.

He continued slowly along the streets, eventually coming to the open space near the main gate. Kingsmen were loitering at the headquarters, watching the young women walking to and from the market. A wagon, drawn by two horses, was coming in the gate. Several riders and another wagon were heading out. Artama fell in with them. The Kingsmen on the towers were watching, but they showed no interest. Along with the others, Artama continued riding away calmly. *Kora should be at the stable by now. There will be more riders and wagons by the time she arrives at the gate. No one will notice.* He increased the pace and began moving beyond the other riders. When he passed the wagon, he took Lightning into a trot. He looked back, saw everyone else still moving slowly, and took Lightning into a canter. Then a gallop.

Artama was caught in the inexorable rush of events. *A twig in a raging river.* He felt like a spectator. Lightning's hooves kicked up a pastel cloud. In all of infinity and eternity, Artama knew he was drawing closer to a transcendental moment. Nothing would ever be the same. An electric current surged up his spine. As Lightning galloped, the air rushed over Artama's face, and his eyes teared. Clenching his teeth, Artama grimaced.

At last, Artama could see dust rising ahead of him on the road. He spurred Lightning. Now, Artama could faintly see a splash of red through the dust. He rode past The Berry, rapidly gaining on the cloud. Now, he could clearly see Tribb's blood-red capote flowing from his shoulders. Artama threw the blanket off the scabbard, and it sailed away in the trailing dust.

Tribb and Hape looked back, spurring and kicking their horses, but the packhorse slowed them. Artama quickly rode up to—and then alongside—Tribb. The Kingsman glared at Artama and viciously spurred his horse. Then, understanding it was useless, he drew rein sharply and came to a stop. Hape did the same. Artama stopped and turned back, facing Tribb, blocking his way. The two men stared at each other, their horses heaving. Hape warily moved his mount and the packhorse off to the right, to the edge of the road.

Tribb shouted, "Move! Out of my way!"

Artama advanced.

"I said move!"

Artama moved—closer.

"I command you to move away, to let us pass!"

Artama smiled.

"Again, I am on The King's business."

"And what business is that?"

"Those writings." Tribb gestured with his thumb toward the packhorse.

Hape was inching forward.

"Those are not yours," Artama said.

"They are evidence . . . evidence of your violations of The King's decree. I am taking them to D'anor."

"But I cannot allow that."

"It is not your decision to make."

The wind began to gust.

"Those writings are for the good of the people, not for the power of D'anor. I will not let you pass with them."

"You are a criminal."

"And you think you can arrest me?"

"I will kill you." Tribb drew his sword and charged.

Artama drew The Crystal and raised it.

The shimmering blade panicked Tribb's horse, and, abruptly, it stopped, rearing violently, throwing him. Now, in the dust, he scrambled to his feet. The horse bolted. In a screaming rage, Tribb ran toward Artama and slashed Lightning's throat—blood spurted, spraying the air. The horse stood for a moment and then collapsed. Artama leaped to the ground, keeping his feet. The two men stood, looking at one another. Tribb was spattered with horse blood. His sword was red. Lightning lay in a growing pool of blood, twitching . . . shuddering . . . then still. Well off the road in the direction of The Honeycomb, Tribb's horse stopped running.

Tribb began to circle to his right.

So did Artama.

At the side of the road, Hape moved slowly forward.

Looking past Tribb, Artama could see Hape and the packhorse and—in the distance—Tribb's horse standing in the dust. Hape opened one of the saddlebags and removed a handful of writings. He threw the sheets into the air, and they began to float and blow away. He took another handful and scattered them into a gust of wind.

Tribb hesitated, staring at the distortions in the air caused by The Crystal.

Beyond Tribb, Artama could see his writings blowing away against the brilliant blue sky, slicing lemniscates in the air.

"Damn you!" Tribb snarled. "They were right . . . about the blade."

Hape took two saddlebags from the packhorse and threw them over his saddle in front of him. He dumped another one—more sheets swirling in the wind. Hape slapped the packhorse on a hindquarter, and they trotted away.

Tribb saw Artama was distracted, and he attacked.

Artama parried. Sparks of blue and gold and white exploded from the blades.

Writings were blowing away.

"Stop this!" Artama shouted.

But Tribb continued his attack.

Artama defended himself exquisitely.

Tribb stepped back.

"Stop!" Artama shouted again.

But—desperately—Tribb attacked.

Artama drove The Crystal into Tribb's stomach—up to the hilt.

Tribb's eyes opened wide in bewilderment.

Hape kicked his horse, galloping away madly.

Tribb's eyes closed for a moment, then reopened—bewilderment became realization.

Artama pulled The Crystal out of Tribb's stomach. Now, the blade was clearly visible—shimmering blood-red.

Tribb collapsed on the road, groveling and moaning in the dust. His eyes closed, and he saw Cressa—slender yet becoming a woman. He heard the river raging. Saw the scarf—a red rope drawn tight, biting into the corners of her mouth. She was face down in the dust—the scarf knotted tightly at the back of her head. She was gagging. He yanked her head back and put his dagger to her throat. She began to sob.

He saw Korbin inside the prisoner's wagon, lying on his side, curled in feculent straw. He saw Korbin on the floor at the feet of D'anor, hair matted and greasy, face bruised and crusted with dried blood.

Tribb tried to get to his knees but slumped face down in the dust, a pool of blood growing around him.

Tribb watched the soldier reach inside the black box, grab Korbin by his hair, drag him out, and dump him on the ground. Still holding him by the hair, the soldier lifted Korbin's head for the crowd to behold. Korbin had no face. Cressa was weeping, and she was not alone. Cressa emerged from the crowd and continued walking—without hesitation—until she reached Korbin. She set her basket on the ground and knelt close to him. Korbin tried to rise, eyes wild. Cressa bent forward and embraced his head, lowering it gently, holding it against her thighs.

Without a horse, Artama stood in the dust, watching Hape ride away.

Artama laid The Crystal on the ground at Tribb's feet, then he turned and quietly walked to the packhorse. He whispered, took the lead, and guided the horse off the road, away from the blood. He whispered again.

Leaving the packhorse standing at the edge of the road, Artama began retrieving as many sheets of writings as he could. Most had blown away, too scattered to pursue. Time was critical. *Hape will tell D'anor, and he will send troops. Hide the writings and get to the tower.* He moved purposefully, gathering sheets of lapa as he worked his way toward Tribb's horse. At last, he reached the animal, whispered to it, took the reins, and stroked its neck. The horse snorted, shivered, and then lowered its head and rubbed against Artama. Artama stuffed the sheets he had collected into a saddlebag. Then, walking, he led the horse toward the packhorse. As he walked, he saw four large birds—scabbies—circling over Lightning and Tribb. One of the birds swooped down and began pecking at the horse's eyes.

The other three swooped down and began pecking at Tribb's eyes and lips. They squabbled briefly, but soon—after changing positions—they settled into eating. Artama stopped by the packhorse, spoke gently to both horses, and then left them standing together. He removed the scabbard from Lightning and retrieved The Crystal. The feasting birds were undisturbed. Flies covered Tribb's face and abdomen. Tribb's bladder and bowels were seeping into the pool of his blood.

Artama dropped to his knees and vomited in the dust.

AS WARM AIR RISES, *water vapor cools, forming a cloud.*

The temperature at the top of the cloud is below freezing—vapor turns to ice.

Rising droplets of water collide with particles of ice. In the collisions, electrons are torn free. Lighter, positively charged particles rise to the top of the cloud. Heavier, negatively charged particles sink to the bottom.

On the surface of the planet, beneath the cloud, a positive charge develops. The imbalance between the cloud and the surface is resolved when negative charges surging downward meet positive charges surging upward, creating a bolt of lightning many times hotter than the surface of the sun.

Heat creates ice, and ice creates fire.

14

DUST FILLED THE AIR, and the setting sun was blood-red, as Artama rode into The Honeycomb, leading the packhorse.

A cave would be best.

The Honeycomb was a wasteland, a vast expanse of escarpments—bleached by the sun—and countless barren caves. Few people willingly ventured there. Hidden, the writings should be safe.

Will they be found? Who will find them? To what end? I need sleep. And I will need a fresh horse.

+++++

Travelers heading from The Capital toward Eastedge came upon the carnage—a dead Kingsman lay in a pool of blood, his eyes devoured and his lips missing, grotesquely exposing his teeth in a ghastly smile. In another pool of blood lay the carcass of a horse, swarming with flies.

The travelers rode straight to The Berry.

Among the few patrons inside the inn, three Kingsmen were seated at a table near the bar, eating and drinking . . . and flirting with the serving wench.

The travelers burst in, shouting over one another.

"Blood is everywhere!"

"On the road!"

"A Kingsman is dead!"

The soldiers jumped to their feet, and the young woman fled.

"Murdered!"

"A sword to the gut!"

"And a horse dead with a slit throat!"

+++++

Artama squinted against the blowing dust as he came to where the caves began. Tribb's horse—a warhorse—moved on steadily. The packhorse was difficult.

Artama began considering caves. He knew it would be better to go deeper into The Honeycomb, farther away from the road, but he needed to make a choice soon, before dark. Everything began looking the same, and he struggled to notice landmarks and memorize his route.

His only possibility for a fresh horse would be The Berry. He wished he could ride to Eastedge and tell Valdar where the writings were hidden, but he would never see Eastedge again. He needed to ride straight to the watchtower. As much as he did not want to implicate Canter, he would need his help.

As Artama made his way through a narrowing pass, he spotted a cave above him. It would take effort to climb to it, making it unlikely that anyone else ever would. He stopped and dismounted. In the pass, there was not much wind or swirling dust. The horses were calm.

+++++

Inside The Berry, The Kingsman in charge, a corporal, gave orders: "Everyone stay here. My men and I will handle this."

Hearing the commotion, Canter came from the kitchen.

"Canter, you come with us," commanded the corporal.

The four men left the inn and ran to the road. At the scene, they stopped . . . and stood transfixed. Dust was sticking to the coagulated blood. The flies were ravenous.

In disbelief, the youngest private said, "Tribb?"

They stood in silence.

Finally, the corporal spoke: "Canter, have my horse—and Private Thane's horse—prepared. And we will need a cart and a horse for young Private Brock. I will leave immediately for The Capital with the news. Thane, you ride to Eastedge, to headquarters, and alert them. Brock, you take the body to The Capital." Then, turning to Canter, he added, "Get this dead horse off the road and out of sight."

+++++

Artama climbed to the cave entrance. He surveyed the vast expanse of other entrances. This one would be good. He looked inside, stepped in, and walked until he reached the darkness. *This will work.* Artama exited the cave and returned to the horses. He removed the saddlebags and the bundles of writings. Climbing was difficult. He made four trips, stacking everything just inside the entrance. Before his final climb, Artama made certain the horses were secured. He took a blanket roll from behind the saddle of Tribb's horse. In the cave, he took the bags and bundles back into the darkness. In a depression in the floor, he stacked the writings, gathered loose rocks, and piled them on top. It would be dry here, and the rocks should protect the writings from varmints.

Now, he needed to rest. He wrapped the blanket around him, sat on the floor of the cave, and leaned against the wall. *Is Kora safe? Will the writings be safe?*

+++++

Deep in the night, Hape arrived at The Capital. His horse was exhausted. Hape could barely stay in the saddle. He rode slowly toward the gate. From a tower, a guard yelled, "Halt!"

Hape was more than happy to comply.

"Who goes there?"

"I am Hape. I have ridden without stopping from Eastedge. I must see The King."

The guard laughed.

"It is of the gravest importance. A Kingsman has been murdered."

Another guard shouted, "Who has been murdered?"

"Tribb!"

"What did you say?"

"Tribb was murdered. Artama murdered Tribb."

"Stay where you are."

Hape waited in the silence. Eventually, one of the large doors opened enough to allow a Kingsman on horseback to pass. The soldier held a lantern in one hand and a sword in the other. He rode toward Hape. "Raise your hands and keep them up."

Hape obeyed.

"You are saying that Artama killed Tribb?"

"Yes, sir. Tribb and I were bringing important papers to The King. Artama stopped us. There was a fight. Swords. Artama killed Tribb."

"Artama killed Tribb?"

"Yes."

The guard was confounded. "Papers? What papers?"

"Artama's writings."

"What writings?"

"Artama has been writing . . . secretly. His papers threaten The Kingdom. D'anor must be told. I have some of them. I can show you. But Artama has bundles of them, and he is escaping. We have no time to lose."

"Put your hands down. Show me."

Hape removed a few sheets from one of the saddlebags in front of him and held them out toward the soldier.

The Kingsman sheathed his sword, took the papers, and held them close to the lantern. He grimaced. The words made no sense to him.

Hape repeated, "Artama is escaping. We must stop him. He killed Tribb, and he is fleeing with the writings."

The guard shouted to The Kingsman in the tower, "Get two men to replace us! Then alert The Night Captain! I will bring this one—*Hape*—to The Captain's office. Go!"

+++++

A buzzing fly woke Artama.

He had been dreaming of the red storm—the first time he saw the dragons—remembering the terrifying, whining sound.

He remembered he had killed Tribb. He saw Tribb's bewildered expression and the flies settling on his coagulating blood. Artama was angry with himself—disappointed. Others would cheer him, but he felt he had murdered his message. Then, again, he knew it was his destiny.

He realized he was praying . . . praying for Kora's safety. He remembered the first time he saw her at the golden fountain, filling a jar with water. The water was silver in the sunlight.

+++++

Hape was sitting on a bench, drinking water, when The Night Captain strode into the office. After a moment, The Night Captain said, "I know you."

"Yes, sir."

"Tell me about it—tell me about Artama, Tribb, and these papers." The Night Captain waved the sheets of lapa he had been given and then tossed them on his desk.

Hape repeated everything.

The Night Captain thought for a while. He studied the sheets. He looked at Hape. Then, without a word, he stood and left the room.

+++++

The fly settled on Artama's cheek. He brushed it away.

Artama recalled the first time he saw Zortan: There was an oily stench in the air. Heavy gold chains—gaudy, mismatched, and chaotic—tangled, twisted, and knotted—hung around Zortan's neck. His face was disfigured by a terrible scar—a scar from fire—down his left temple and cheek. His left eye was partially closed by the damage.

+++++

At last, Hape was taken to The Chamber. The Night Captain, The Jester, and The Commander General were already there. Each held sheets of the writings.

The Jester, in grim make-up, spoke, "We are told that Artama has been secretly writing and that these writings—besides being illegal—may be threatening to The Kingdom." Hape started to respond, but The Jester interrupted, "And we have been told that Artama killed Tribb . . . in a sword fight."

"Yes."

The Jester resumed, "The papers I can see, but I find it hard to believe that Artama could defeat Tribb in a sword fight."

Hape did not know the protocol for addressing The Jester, so he just began speaking. "I saw it. He had a sword with an invisible blade. And he is amazingly skilled. It was quick."

"The tales and songs are true?"

"Yes."

"And the writings?"

"Not only do they call into question the authority of The King and The High Priest, but they contain information about weapons of unimaginable power. With such weapons, Artama could defeat the army . . . he could overthrow The King."

"You have seen enough of these writings to know that?"

"Yes, and he confided in me."

"And where is he?"

"I last saw him near Crossroads, near The Berry. But he will be fleeing to a tower on

The Plain he told me about. He calls this tower a *portal*. If he gets there, we will never see him again. I do not know what he will do with the writings . . . he may take them with him . . . he may give them to someone . . . he may hide them. We need to stop him . . . and we are wasting time."

The Jester looked to The High Priest.

The High Priest looked to The Commander General.

The Commander General looked to The Night Captain and said, "Wake The King."

The Night Captain flinched. "Sir?"

"See that The King is awakened immediately."

+++++

Artama rolled to his left side and, eventually, fell asleep. He dreamed of the night he saw The Game for the first time: There was a circle of beastly men, and, in the center of the circle, a young man wearing a black leather helmet with reptilian spikes—dragon-spikes—running down from the crown. The young man wore black leather gloves, and he crouched beside a blazing fire—red and orange and yellow. A dirty black cloud boiled into the night. The men in the circle threw glowing coals at the man in the center, and he batted them away—or caught them and threw them back in his own attack.

The fly landed on Artama's hand, on Tribb's dried blood. Artama flicked his wrist, and the fly flew away.

+++++

The Night Captain made his way through the halls of The Palace until he came to the door of The Matron. He knocked and waited. He knocked again . . . and waited. In time, the door opened enough that The Matron and The Night Captain could look into each other's eyes. The Night Captain's eyes were wide. The Matron's were squinted.

"What is it?" she asked.

"You must wake The King."

"What?"

"You must wake The King—by order of The Commander General. He is needed in The Chamber."

The Matron nodded. "Understood." She closed the door.

There were three doorways into The King's bedroom: the royal doorway (through which The King passed formally), the escape doorway (through which he could make his way secretly down a stairway and eventually into a labyrinth of tunnels), and a frequently used doorway for the concubines. The Matron knocked on the latter door. She waited. Knocked again, louder. Waited. Knocked again. The door opened. A beautifully disheveled young woman stood inside, looking confused.

"Out!" shouted The Matron, snapping her fingers and waving her hand.

The concubine ran.

The Matron entered the bedroom and went to the bed of The King. Only faint moonlight came through the window. The King was lying on his stomach, asleep, passed out.

The Matron nudged him. Waited. Shook him gently. D'anor groaned. She shook him again. "My Lord, you must wake up." He groaned again. "You must wake up. You are needed." The King rolled over. His night mask was pushed askew, and the bottom half of his horrid face was exposed. He straightened the mask and rose on one elbow. In a drunken slur, he said, "What?"

"All I know is The Commander General needs you in The Chamber."

"Damn!"

"May I be of any help, My Lord?"

"No. Go."

The Matron left the room.

The King swung his feet over the edge of the bed and sat motionless, trying to collect his thoughts.

+++++

The fly landed on Artama's lips, and he awoke with a start.

In the darkness, he remembered climbing the tower, working carefully, hand

and foot. As he climbed, the sky became a brighter, angry red. He felt a sharp pain in his back. And then another. He could not breathe. He could hear Zortan's guards taunting him—as they threw rocks. Artama was climbing for his life. He struggled to find holds and steps. A rock hit his right hand, almost costing him his grip. And then, at the cosmic moment when Artama turned his head, a rock hit, splitting open the center of his forehead—a bursting red star of torn flesh—sending blood swirling in the air.

Artama could only endure. Beyond that, he was helpless. But if he endured, he could climb beyond the threat of the rocks, beyond the power of the guards.

At last, he reached the top of the tower and crawled over a low wall of rocks on the rim. On the other side, he leaned back against the wall. Blood was running down onto his nose and cheeks. He wiped it away and wiped his bloody hand on his leg.

Finally, he was safe, and although he could hear the guards cursing, it was almost quiet.

He could think.

Now, in the darkness in the cave, he remembered the dragons as they flew straight toward the tower—an undulating swarm of ancient, fire-breathing, reptilian creatures. Crouched among the rocks at the edge of the tower, Artama watched as the swarm flew directly over him. The first dragons were small, with keen red eyes. Their wings were translucent, fast, and generated a high-pitched whine. Quick and agile. Smoke blew back from their nostrils and fire torched from their mouths. They had fierce talons. But their eyesight was their power.

Following the dragons with red eyes were larger dragons—dragons with yellow eyes. Their wings were thicker membranes. They, too, had flaming mouths. But their power was in their talons: brutal, ripping, shredding blades. The whining became a deeper, humming despair.

Then came the true dragons of fire, dragons with blue eyes—gargantuan creatures that could produce almost invisible heat.

And Artama witnessed the blessed, terrifying destruction of Zortan's horde.

+++++

The Ministers of Information, Education, Commerce, Law, and The Treasury were now in The Chamber, along with The High Priest, The Commander General, The Night Captain, and The Jester.

The King entered The Chamber through the royal doorway and made his way unsteadily to The Throne. He seated himself and, with effort, straightened and sat erect. He was wearing his war-council mask. "What is this about?"

The Jester spoke, "Hape has brought news from Eastedge. He says Artama has killed Tribb. He says Artama has been writing extensively and has written blasphemous

273

material, material threatening to you and The Kingdom, material about secret weaponry that could enable a defeat of the army. Hape confiscated these writings and was bringing them to you—with the help of Tribb—when Artama stopped them. There was a sword fight, and Artama killed Tribb. Hape, with some of the papers, arrived here in the night. He says Artama is fleeing with bundles and bundles of these writings."

"What kind of weaponry?" asked D'anor.

"According to Hape, Artama calls them *explosives*," said The Commander General. "More powerful than any storm of nature. One weapon can throw more fire than a thousand dragons."

The Jester spoke, "Hape says Artama will escape unless we—"

"Where is Hape?" demanded The King.

The Commander General said, "Waiting in the antechamber."

"Get him in here."

The Night Captain went immediately to the main door, opened it, and demanded Hape.

Hape came through the doorway and dropped to his knees. "My Lord, I bring grave news."

"So, I am told. Come forward."

Hape rose and walked to within ten feet of The Throne. "My Lord, you must act now. Artama is escaping, most likely heading for what he calls a *portal*. I have never been there, but he talked about it. It is a tower on The Plain. I can give you directions and a description. He may take the writings with him. He may give them to someone else. He may hide them."

The King shouted, "I want the writings, and I want Artama!" D'anor was fully alert now. Addressing Hape, The King said, "Where did this killing take place?"

"At Crossroads, near The Berry."

D'anor turned to The Commander General. "Take a platoon. Organize three patrols. Send one to Crossroads and begin a search for anything you can find. Question everyone. He most likely will go into The Honeycomb. He may go to The Berry. Send a second patrol to Eastedge. Capture his so-called wife. If we have her, we will have him. And Commander, you lead the third patrol to this *portal*, wherever—*whatever*—that is. Take Hape for guidance. I want Artama caught, and I want him alive. Once we begin torturing him—and his damned whore—he will tell us everything we need to know. And I want to kill them both—*myself*. Go! Leave! Now!"

+++++

Artama rolled to his right side, dreaming. At Kora's favorite place, he stepped onto the low stone wall. Naked, facing the pool, he stood for a moment, took a deep breath, then dived into the water. The pool was delightfully comfortable, neither cool nor warm: perfect. Kora rolled over and submerged again. Under the water, their eyes met in deep vision. Everything was flowing crystal at the edge. Lost in Kora's eyes, Artama saw his earth orbiting his sun, and he saw the dragon moon orbiting . . . .

The fly settled on his cheek. Artama roused.

The night seemed interminable. Artama wanted—needed—to be on his way, but he needed a fresh, strong horse. He needed to stop at The Berry, but it would be foolish to arouse attention in the middle of the night. He needed to wait until dawn—when activity at the inn would naturally begin.

In time, Artama drifted into a dream of the bandits on The Plain. He drew The Cystal from the scabbard on his back. The bandits began to circle him, and Artama turned with them. The interplay of forces . . . orbiting. They stopped. The bandits attacked. There was a flurry of rapid cracking sounds and a fury of bright flashes . . . and then Artama was blinded by an unimaginable flash of light. When he recovered his sight, he saw Kora— translucent, gossamer. Dark eyes radiantly ethereal. Dark hair floating in stardust.

The fly landed on his forehead.

Artama awoke, remembering his father's final words: "You have shown the way. You have done all you can do."

Artama swatted the fly, killing it.

At long last, a whisper of light was visible at the entrance to the cave.

It is time.

THE FATHER *determines the sex of the offspring—providing an X or Y chromosome. A single gene—SRY—on the Y chromosome signals the developmental pathway. The double helix, the two antiparallel strands of DNA, carry the genetic instructions.*

And so, the path of a humanoid begins— a boy with characteristics of a father who crossed The Plain and visited another world . . . and attributes of a mother who was born on another world and traveled to save the father.

15

BREAKING ABOVE THE HORIZON, the sun rose ominously in purple and gold. In contrast to the somber light, the air was fresh and invigorating.

Leading the unburdened packhorse, Artama rode through The Honeycomb, back toward The Berry. From lack of sleep and lying on the floor of the cave, his body ached. He felt like an old man. As he rode, he memorized the route. He knew he would never see the cave again, but he wanted to provide accurate directions, if ever needed. The journey before him was daunting—onto The Plain to the portal . . . and beyond. He rode steadily. Now, in the eternal verisimilitude of time, every moment was precious—a matter of life and death.

+++++

In the malefic morning light, departing The Capital, The Kingsmen began their quest. They rode urgently, with abandon, not comprehending the hardship and ultimate calamity of the journey before them, only knowing they were commanded to stop Artama. Setting the pace, The Commander General himself led the platoon. Swaying In agony, Hape rode at The Commander's side, exhausted from his ride to The Capital and a night without sleep.

+++++

The purple was fading from the sky as Artama emerged from The Honeycomb. He could see The Berry, and he made his way toward it. As he approached, he saw a boy in the corral behind the inn. This would be Artama's first contact after the murder. Disheveled, with dried blood spattered over him, Artama wondered how he would be received? He picked up the pace.

The boy sensed something and looked toward The Honeycomb. He saw the rider approaching, leading another horse without a rider. Dust was rising behind them. The boy stood watching, wondering who would be riding out of The Honeycomb at dawn?

Artama saw the boy standing still, forsaking his chores. Artama raised his right hand and gave a reassuring wave.

Watching the horses canter across the dust, the boy walked to the gate and opened it.

Artama rode inside and stopped.

The boy closed the gate, turned, looked up at Artama, and saw the spattered, dried blood. Astonished, the boy looked directly into Artama's eyes.

Artama said, "Son, you must be a man. Tell Canter Artama is here. Say nothing more to anyone."

The boy turned and ran.

Surely, by now, Hape has told D'anor he can lead The Kingsmen to the tower.

Canter appeared in the doorway at the back of the inn, the boy close beside him.

Artama raised his right hand.

Canter told the boy, "Stay here."

Artama dismounted as Canter walked toward him. When the innkeeper was close, Artama said, "I am sorry to burden you."

"What can I do?"

"I will need your best horse—fast and durable. You will never see it again."

Without hesitation, Canter said, "I will give you Thunder. He is my best. I will instruct the boy to gather water and food. I will prepare the horse. Stay here. We will be quick. There were Kingsmen here, but they have gone—we are safe . . . for now."

"Thank you, Canter. To replace Thunder—and more—see Brax. I will be gone . . . forever."

"I need no compensation. Knowing you is a blessing. Artama, you will be missed . . . but never forgotten."

+++++

The Kingsmen rode furiously, without thought of preserving their horses, and by midday, they arrived at Crossroads. At the order of The

Commander, one patrol rode into The Honeycomb, another continued toward Eastedge, and The Commander's patrol rode to The Berry.

+++++

Artama knew The Kingsmen would ride hard. He would need to push, yet he had to spare his horse. He had the advantage of knowing the way, and he knew where he could safely depart from the direct route and find precious water. Unfortunately, he had no experience with his mount, but he had faith in Canter—Thunder would be a warrior.

Time would tell.

+++++

At The Berry, The Commander demanded fresh horses. While the change was being accomplished, The Kingsmen questioned everyone—Canter, the stable boy, the kitchen help and serving wenches, Canter's wife and daughter, and the guests eating lunch. No one knew anything about Artama. They had only heard that Tribb had been killed.

When the horses were ready, The Commander immediately led his patrol toward The Plain in pursuit of Artama.

+++++

In The Honeycomb, The Kingsmen searched, listlessly, more or less randomly, for Artama. They knew it was a hopeless task. As the sun lowered and the light eventually began to fade—as their fruitless efforts dragged on— they began thinking about a comfortable night in The Berry (the food, the wine, the women, and a bed). They knew they were the lucky ones.

+++++

In the darkness, the Eastedge patrol arrived and went directly to the headquarters. The chest, neck, and sides of the horses were slick with sweat—white lather. Their heads were hanging, nostrils flaring with each breath, wide eyes rolling or almost closed. Several swayed, a restless hoof moving to maintain balance. After a brief discussion, two Eastedge soldiers joined the exhausted patrol and led the way to Artama's cottage.

When they arrived, the two soldiers dismounted, went to the front door, and began banging on it, shouting, "Open up!" They pounded and shouted, "By order of The King, open the door!"

No answer.

"Kora! Open the door!"

No response.

The leader of the patrol commanded, "Break it down!"

Together, the two soldiers heaved against it, and after several attempts, the door burst open.

The leader shouted, "Inside! Everyone! Bring her out!"

Eventually, the soldiers emerged.

"No one."

"Empty."

The leader spat. "Damn her!"

+++++

Artama was lying in the darkness, staring at the dragon moon as it moved beneath the innumerable stars, thinking of Kora, wondering if he would ever see her again. He knew The Kingsmen would drive their horses—they could afford to lose some. He had no idea how many soldiers would pursue him, but there would most likely be many. He knew they would gain on him. He had to care for Thunder, for Thunder was his only hope. It was cold, but he could not risk the light of a fire. He was exhausted but unable to sleep—his thoughts swirled. Slowly, the dragon moon traversed the firmament. Artama felt terribly alone . . . far away . . . far away from everything.

+++++

Hape and The Kingsmen, wrapped in their blankets, were lying near a fire, sleeping. Hape was snoring. Occasionally, one of the soldiers would grunt and jerk an arm or kick spasmodically. The Commander General, wrapped in his blanket, watched the dragon moon slowly move across the sky. He knew numbers were in his favor: He could lose horses and men—he had only to capture *one* man—damned Artama. They would ride before the break of dawn.

+++++

Artama awoke with a jolt. The sun was up, already entirely above the horizon. He knew he was in trouble.

+++++

The Commander General, Hape, and the soldiers were riding hard toward the rising sun.

+++++

Throughout the agonizing day, Artama varied his pace—sometimes pushing Thunder, sometimes slowing to a walk. Now, he was stopped, dismounted, allowing Thunder a brief rest. He tightened the cinch.

Artama looked to the west—into the late afternoon sky—and he saw the sight he dreaded—dust rising in the distance. *Closing on me. Now, they can undoubtedly follow my tracks.* He mounted Thunder and was quickly at a gallop, riding in a fury over the uneven ground. This horse was fearless. There was hope.

Artama remembered Kora singing to him by the pool on his last night on E1:

> *I came for you.*
>
> *I came for anyone in pain,*
>
> *And you know I return,*
>
> *And you know I remain.*
>
> *I remember uneven ground . . .*
>
> *Men looking for gold,*
>
> *Looking for power,*
>
> *Looking in vain.*
>
> *And fallen on the uneven ground*
>
> *Were men without gold,*
>
> *Without power,*
>
> *Burning,*
>
> *Crying in vain.*
>
> *I came for you.*
>
> *I came for anyone in pain,*

And you know I return,

And you know I remain . . .

One Love.

Artama looked back. The cloud of dust behind him was closer. Thunder was galloping at his limit. Artama looked ahead. Dust began to rise before him—swirling in a fresh wind—and his eyes began to water. He thought he could see the watchtower.

Artama heard a gruesome snap, and Thunder collapsed, horse and rider lurching toward the ground. Time slowed . . . rocks and dust came toward Artama, and he landed on his face and chest. The horse rolled onto its back, kicking in the air, and then rolled over Artama and lay on its side, twitching. Artama lay on the ground, unable to breathe, descending into unconsciousness.

Valiantly, Thunder struggled to stand . . . in vain.

Artama heard the hum of electricity and the voice of Kora singing:

You fell—

And felt forsaken—
On the white stone,
Where the wind blew everywhere.

Dust filled the air.
The light began to fade,
But you are not alone.

Artama began breathing. He found he could move his arms and legs. At last, he managed to stand.

Thunder was on his side, quivering. His right front leg grotesquely twisted.

Artama limped to Thunder and managed to remove The Crystal from its scabbard. Gripping the sword, he stood for a moment with his head lowered. *You are not alone.* He heard horses in the distance. In the swirling wind, he made two deep cuts into Thunder's throat, blood spraying into the dust. *Who will slit my throat?* He slid The Crystal—the blade garishly visible with blood—inside his belt.

Slowly, at first, Artama started for the watchtower. Soon, he was running for his life.

+++++

The Kingsmen stopped briefly at the bloody carcass of the horse. Flies were already feasting. With the bloodlust of Zortan's horde, the soldiers raged onward.

+++++

Now, Artama could hear the shouts of The Kingsmen clearly. He turned, and he could see them.

But the watchtower was near. He could make it!

He ran like a madman, and at last, he stumbled to the base of the tower.

On his hands and knees, he looked around.

The rope is gone! She must have pulled it up . . . after she climbed.

The Commander General screamed: "Stop him!"

And then, the rope came flying from the top of the tower.

Artama shouted, "Kora!"

Kora's head appeared above the wall of rocks. "I waited!"

An arrow hit the tower beside him . . . rock splintering.

Another arrow hit . . . just to his left.

And then overhead, a dragon appeared out of the swirling dust—a dragon with red eyes—leading an undulating swarm of ancient, reptilian creatures. Smoke blew back from their nostrils, and fire torched from their mouths.

Hape was the first to turn his horse to flee.

The Commander General screamed again: "Stop Artama!"

Two Kingsmen shot arrows, but the others fled, following Hape.

Following the red-eyed dragon were larger creatures with yellow eyes and flaming mouths . . . and brutal, ripping, shredding talons.

Aided by the rope, Artama began climbing.

A yellow-eyed dragon torched Hape, and he fell from his horse in flames . . . screaming . . . writhing on the ground.

All The Kingsmen were now fleeing—except one who remained beside The Commander General. The Kingsman raised his bow and took aim.

There was a brilliant burst of dragon-fire and an instantaneous vaporization of flesh. For a moment, the skeleton of The Kingsman sat upon the skeleton of his horse, then both collapsed into glowing ashes on the dust.

Desperately, viciously, hatefully, The Commander General spurred his horse toward the tower, wielding his sword above his head.

From above, Kora watched in horror. She stepped back, gripped the rope, leaned back, pulled with all her might, and pushed with all the strength of her legs.

The Commander General slashed, but Artama was lifted out of reach, and The Commander's sword futilely severed the rope just below Artama's feet.

A dragon dropped onto The Commander General and sank its talons into him. Carrying its prey, the dragon soared into the sky, spiraling higher and higher.

Artama reached the top of the tower, and Kora helped him over the wall. They watched in awe as the true dragons of fire, the dragons with blue eyes—the gargantuan creatures that could produce almost invisible heat—flew overhead . . . and then dived and vaporized everything on the ground. The stench was miasmic.

High above the tower, the dragon discarded The Commander General. He plummeted—flailing and screaming—until he hit the edge of the top of the tower, broke apart in a burst of blood and flesh and bones, and fell to the ground in a dismembered heap.

Artama and Kora heard the light before they saw the sound. Ozone blurred their vision. The humming was a deep, electric, reverberant, magnetic sensation . . . an ethereal resonance, a vibration of opalescent, translucent colors beyond the humanoid spectrum. Artama remembered the colors of the vibrations of the meteoron strings—the visual, tactile tones of the cosmos. He was breathing rapidly, heart pounding. He turned to Kora and looked into her unfathomable, dark eyes . . . now glistening with silver tears. Her dark hair floating in stardust. He remembered her standing by the golden fountain of silver water glistening in the sunlight. He inhaled the fragrance . . . the fragrance he knew and loved . . . the fragrance of miraculous healing . . . . He heard the cosmic chorus, the reverberating song everlasting . . . felt the purity of the harmony . . . and from within the chorus, he heard Kora speak his name. Exhilarating warmth coursed his spine . . . . He knew eternity.

Within a magnificently bright burst of light, Artama and Kora—entangled in a rapturous embrace—ascended into the blue and gold and white.

***IN SUPERPOSITION**, anything probabilistically exists, ready to materialize at the moment of observation. Observation causes the probabilistic wavefunction to collapse, and the object emerges in a location. When two particles are born from one—entanglement—as when light is directed into a crystal and one violet photon becomes two red photons, moving separately but sharing the same wavefunction—when one is observed, its wavefunction and that of its mate simultaneously collapse, regardless of the distance between them, even to the limit of the universe. Neither space nor time exists. They demonstrate complementary characteristics . . . and they appear to know.*